THE CONSTANTINE ANCHOR CROSS

Richard G. Edwards

Copyright @ 2016 Richard G. Edwards

ISBN XXX-X-XXX-XXXX-X

All rights reserved. No part of this publication may be reproduced, stored in a retrieval system, or transmitted in any form or by any means, electronic, mechanical, recording or otherwise, without the prior written permission of the author.

Published by EMTCC, LLC, Lexington, Kentucky

Printed in the United States of America on acid-free paper.

The characters and events in this book are fictitious. Any similarity to real persons, living or dead, is coincidental and not intended by the author.

EMTCC, LLC
2016

First Edition

Cover Photos

The two photographs on the cover were taken by the author. The top photo is of the Pantheon in Rome, Italy. The bottom photo is a view of Harlan, Kentucky taken from Ivy Hill.

Acknowledgments

I wish to sincerely thank my wife Carolyn, Dr. Carl Peters, Dr. August Peters, Dr. Bill Green, Mrs. Brita Seybert, and Mr. Jack Sterling for taking the time and expending the effort to review this book. I greatly appreciate their doing so. Mrs. Kelly Elliott was responsible for the layout of all five books in my Anchor Cross Series. It was a true pleasure to work with her.

Dedication

My wife Carolyn and I were married on April 2, 1966. Lord permitting, we will celebrate our 50th wedding anniversary this year. I dedicate this final book in the Anchor Cross Series to my lovely, loving, and devoted wife, Carolyn. It's been a great half century together…..Pax Tecum!

Preface

If you have read any of my previous Anchor Cross books, ***The Anchor Cross*** (now also available as ***The Anchor Cross Second Edition***), ***The Pelle Anchor Cross***, ***The Helena Anchor Cross***, or ***The Anchor Cross Twins***, you are aware that the theme of the books revolve about six anchor crosses that were cast by Roman Emperor Constantine the Great in 325 A.D. using gold that was traced back to being blessed by my Lord Jesus Christ and then given to Saint Peter to help start the church. ***The Constantine Anchor Cross*** continues with that theme. I would encourage my readers to share their thoughts and comments with me. My email address is:

richardglennedwards@gmail.com

If you would like copies of my previous Anchor Cross books, please either contact me at the above email address, or you may order them from:

www.BookLocker.com — ***The Anchor Cross***
www.Amazon.com — ***The Anchor Cross***
The Anchor Cross Second Edition
The Pelle Anchor Cross
The Helena Anchor Cross
The Anchor Cross Twins
www.BarnesandNoble.com — ***The Anchor Cross***
The Anchor Cross Second Edition
The Pelle Anchor Cross
The Helena Anchor Cross
The Anchor Cross Twins

May God Bless, and Pax Tecum!

Chapter 1

Key West, Florida

Teagan and Jackson Lange are divers. Teagan is 36 years old. Her brother Jackson is 34. They grew up on Key Largo in Florida. Their love of the sea started when their family took them on numerous trips to the beach shortly after they were out of diapers. It had continued through the years. They each attended the University of Miami, and received degrees in marine science. After college they moved together to Key West and worked several years for Mel Fisher's various enterprises, first in his museum, and later as divers aboard his treasure-hunting boats. While in Key West they met and became friends with Cooper and Clayton Thomas. The Thomas brothers had started treasure hunting about 10 years ago, first with a small 35-foot-long boat, but had recently purchased a 50 footer after having made a discovery of gold and other artifacts from a sunken Spanish vessel located about 20 miles off Key West. Teagan and Jackson had first met Cooper and Clayton while swimming at a Key West beach where the Thomas brothers also had their sister, Lillie, with them. Lillie served as the business manager for Thomas Salvaging, LLC. The five quickly became good friends and frequently got together to talk about treasure hunting. The Thomas' became convinced they wanted to have Teagan and Jackson join their business, and they had invited the two siblings to their home for dinner. After a wonderful seafood dinner, all were relaxed in the den to talk.

Teagan said, "That dinner was really good. I'm stuffed."

Jackson added, "Yeah, me too. We really do appreciate your kind invitation to come for dinner. Teagan and I have agreed that you three are our very best friends here in Key West. We really admire the three of you. You have done what we would like someday to accomplish....to have our own diving company. We've greatly enjoyed and appreciated working for Mel Fisher's Enterprises, but we think we have reached a point in our careers where we would like to try and make a go of it for ourselves. I know you know what I mean....you've been there and done that."

Cooper Thomas replied, "Are you two mind readers? Clayton, Lillie, and I have had discussions about how we could possibly entice you two to join with us. We feel we know you well, and we know you've very successfully worked for Fisher Enterprises as divers. We know you have a love for the sea and an appetite for finding sunken treasure. Would you consider an offer from us?"

Jackson turned to his sister, Teagan, with an inquisitive look on his face. Teagan smiled and nodded her head affirmatively.

Jackson then said, "I think the possibility of working together has been a mutual thought. Teagan and I have talked several times about how much we looked up to you and what you've been able to accomplish. Unfortunately, we don't have much money to contribute, and for that reason we have never felt comfortable bringing up the subject. So, to answer your question....we would indeed love to consider an arrangement whereby we could work together."

Lillie then said, "Fortunately, with the large treasure we recently found, we're financially in good shape. We really are not looking for capital. What we need are good, experienced divers that we feel comfortable with, and you two fit that bill exactly. What we have in mind is a new location where many old shipwrecks are known to exist. We would be interested to purchase a suitable office and boat for you, and to pay you a salary with a great incentive. We would split any monies you received from recovered treasures. While technically you would be working for Thomas Salvaging, the sky would be the limit."

Teagan responded, "I'm sure I speak for Jackson when I say that we're very humbled by the faith you show in us. Speaking for myself, and I bet for Jackson also, I would be greatly interested to explore the kind of arrangement you suggested. But let me ask, if you know of such a great location, why would you not be interested to just move your operation there?"

Clayton replied, "Mainly because we're already well established here in Key West, and our operations here continue to be very successful. We would like to stay here, but stake you two to open another operation for us."

"How, exactly, would we proceed," Jackson asked.

"We think we know you well enough that a hand shake would be sufficient to allow us to talk particulars," replied Clayton. "I know you would want to know your salary and proposed new location. Can we agree to discuss particulars?"

Teagan and Jackson simultaneously stood up and stuck out their hands. Lillie, Cooper, and Clayton stood and joined in a great hand-shaking. Back slapping and laughter followed each hand shake.

"Okay, okay....I think we're all in agreement, at least in general. Now let's again be seated and let me tell you the particulars," Cooper said.

All were then seated. Cooper first told the Langes what their salary would be. It exceeded their current salary by about 50 percent. Large smiles formed on their faces, and they both nodded in agreement.

Then Cooper went on to address the location, "Have either of you heard of the island of Ponza, or the isola di Ponza?"

The smiles on Teagan and Jackson's faces faded, and they both shook their heads negatively. Teagan said, "No, I don't think we have. I take it from the 'isola di Ponza' that it is likely somewhere around Italy?"

"You are correct," replied Cooper. Ponza is the largest of

the Italian Pontine Islands archipelago. It's located 20 miles south of Cape Circeo in the Tyrrhenian Sea. Ventotene is another somewhat well known island in the Pontines. The islands are located about midway between the cities of Rome and Naples, off the Western Italian coast. In ancient times the island was called Tyrrhenia. There is a legend that says that Ponza is what is left of the lost island of Tyrrhenia. The legend says that Ponza had been connected to the mainland by a narrow strip of land which sank for some reason, leaving Ponza as an island. At any rate, it has a very long history, and many shipwrecks have occurred around the island, dating back to before the time of Christ. Clayton, Lillie, and I vacationed there about five years ago, and were most intrigued by the possibilities for recovering treasure from sunken ships near the island. We have done a lot of research, and have been in contact with various people on Ponza and in the Italian government regarding the possible opening of an office there. Everything we have discovered is very positive."

"What would be the situation with respect to discovering antiquities that would be claimed by the Italian government?" asked Teagan.

Lillie replied, "We would deal with the Italian government's Office of Culture Ministry. Any treasures we find would be reported to the Culture Ministry. They would evaluate them and decide if they wanted to retain ownership. For those retained they would then give us a percentage of their value. My understanding is that they have been more than fair with treasure hunters since they wish to recover more and more antiquities."

Teagan said, "So, have the islanders and the Italian government generally approved your establishing a base on Ponza?"

Clayton replied, "They have. Knowing that we now have a successful operation here in the U.S. has caused them to be very supportive."

Cooper then said, "So, everything looks good to go from our end. We just need the right people to go there, set up operations, and get the show on the road; or, I guess I should say, get the show going under the water. Clayton, Lillie, and I think the two of you are the right people. Ponza is a truly lovely island. There is a great beach there called Chiaia di Luna, and we have even located what looks to be a very lovely little villa close to the beach where you could live. Our office would be at the harbor. We have an agent there who has recommended both the villa and a building that could serve as our office."

"I don't think I'm going to sleep well tonight," Jackson replied. "This is absolutely mind boggling. Just a short time ago Teagan and I were thinking what a wonderful meal we had enjoyed with our dear friends, and now the opportunity of a lifetime is presented to us. Wow!"

Teagan added, "How could we not accept! It's what we do, and it's an opportunity that would be a 'win-win' for all of us. Jackson and I just thank you so very much for placing so much confidence in us. I, for one, vote a big strong YES. We'll take your offer and try to do the best job possible." Teagan then looked at Jackson.

Jackson smiled and said, "As Teagan said, it's an offer made in heaven for us. It sure gets my vote also."

All five friends then stood and engaged in another giant round of handshaking and back slapping. A big trip to Italy was coming up shortly for Teagan and Jackson.

•••

Ponza, Italy
Six months later

The beautiful, turquoise water in the Tyrrhenian Sea lapped at the sides of their dive boat. Teagan had just surfaced from a dive, and the only sound she heard was that of the water slapping the boat. Jackson had killed the boat's engine. It was just gorgeous out here in the water today. The sun blazed down through fluffy white clouds. She pulled her face mask out and placed it up over her forehead. She removed the mouthpiece from her SCUBA gear. She then looked over at the boat and saw her brother, Jackson, grinning at her.

"I can't believe we get paid for doing this," Teagan shouted. "What a job!"

Jackson replied, "Somebody's gotta do it .... may as well be us! Did you see anything of interest this time?"

"Nothing," said Teagan. "Mostly just sand and a few stunning fish. How far have we gone along this sand bar?"

"So far today we've covered about 500 feet," said Jackson. "It's early .... we should be able to cover at least another 500 feet before heading back in."

Teagan was pulling a vacuum hose along the top of a sand bar that had only about 25 feet of water above it. She also had an underwater magnetometer capable of detecting many metals in addition to iron . She would move along the ridge of the sand bar and watch the magnetometer. When she got a positive reading from it, she would stop and use the vacuum hose to suck sand away from the spot where metal was indicated. In most instances she would just uncover some worthless sea debris. Patience and persistence were required. Only about two weeks after she and Jackson began treasure hunting at Ponza she discovered a stretch along the sand bar that contained many gold and silver coins dating back to around the time of Christ. It turned out that the value of the coins was estimated at $800,000. The Culture Ministry paid them $400,000. The Langes kept $200,000 and sent $200,000 to Thomas Salvaging in Key West. All were delighted with this quick discovery.

Thomas Salvaging Ponza, or TSP, had been fully established about one month after Teagan and Jackson arrived. Their villa was even better than advertised, and the office at the harbor was exactly what they needed as a base for their operations. They located a suitable dive boat 10 days after arrival and had managed to get all the required equipment and supplies and settled into their office within the first four weeks. A lot of their time prior to beginning underwater activity was spent studying nautical surface and contour maps and talking with

Ponza natives about areas where shipwrecks were thought to have occurred. They finally decided to concentrate their initial efforts along a shallow sand bar that seemed well positioned to have a reasonably high probability to contain wreckage. Their efforts were well rewarded when after only two weeks they discovered the ancient Roman coins.

The dive boat they acquired was 35 feet long and had a cabin that was suitable for sleeping, cooking, and storage of all their diving gear. Jackson had volunteered to be primarily responsible for the boat, and Teagan was the primary diver, although they agreed that sometimes they would exchange jobs so that each could get additional experience and relieve the other. The arrangement had gone well.

Teagan and Jackson had also quickly learned to greatly appreciate the people of Ponza. The island has a population of just over 3,000 inhabitants. The siblings had found them to be a very friendly and helpful people. Jackson had been a member of Rotary, International, while living in Key West, and he quickly transferred his membership to the Ponza Rotary Club upon moving there. Through Rotary he had met many of the leaders on the island and found them to be most receptive to answer questions that came up. Teagan had always enjoyed painting as a hobby and had located and enrolled in a class that was taught at the library one evening per week. Another hobby she enjoyed was spending time on the computer, and she had discovered a computer special interest group that also met at the library on a different evening from her painting class. Through these two classes she had made many new friends on Ponza.

The past several months had been pretty uneventful in finding sea treasure. Many long days were spent moving slowly along the sand bar. They had located several ceramic antiquities that were contained in wooden boxes with metal strapping and had found several very old and interesting metal pieces that had been parts of old wrecked ships and lots of old anchors and cleats. But the total worth of all their findings since locating the valuable coins had only been evaluated by the Culture Ministry as worth a total of $2400, and they had paid the Langes only $1,000 for them. Half of this was sent to Thomas Salvaging, and so they had netted only $500. They were ready for another real treasure find!

After another week of undersea probing, Teagan had switched jobs with her brother. Jackson was moving slowly along the sand bar, keeping his eyes focused on the magnetometer. Suddenly he saw what appeared as a faint blip, but it did indicate something metallic was there.

He moved the end of the vacuum hose over the area and started to remove sand. After another 10 minutes the vacuum uncovered some kind of box. It was largely wood and in a state of decomposition. Removing more sand from around it revealed it was quite small, perhaps only about 12 inches by 12 inches by about 4 inches thick. It did have several metal bands strapped around it, and there appeared to be hinges on one edge and a small rusty hasp and lock on the opposite side. Jackson carefully removed the box and started heading to the surface with it.

"Find something?" shouted Teagan. She was seated at the helm of the boat with the engine turned off. She had been steering the boat's rudder to follow the air bubbles and vacuum tube from Jackson. There was enough wind to permit the boat to respond very slowly to the helm.

"I did," Jackson shouted back as he removed his face mask and mouthpiece. "Don't know if it's anything....it's kind of small, but I hear good things come in small packages! Who knows?"

"Bring it over and I'll grab it with the net," Teagan replied as she stood and picked up the large fish net.

Jackson swam over to the boat's side and placed the box in the net. Teagan lifted it up on board and removed it from the net.

"It looks old," Teagan said.

"Yeah, I thought so too," replied Jackson. "I think it's been in the water long enough that prying the lock off shouldn't present a problem. I'm tired. I think I'll come aboard for a rest, and we'll see if there's anything in it."

Jackson swam to the back of the boat and pulled up and sat on the dive platform. He took off his SCUBA equipment, mask, and flippers. He then walked onto the deck and joined his sister.

Teagan had already flushed the box using the boat's water hose that received fresh water pumped from the water holding tank. She held the box, clean of all sand but now dripping water.

Jackson looked at it and said, "Well, my curiosity can't take it much longer....why don't we just open up this baby and see what she might hold in store for us!"

Teagan handed her brother the box. Jackson retrieved a screw driver from the boat's tool box and began to pry on the hasp that held the lock. Hasp and lock fell immediately to the deck. He then opened the hinged box top. Once open it became apparent to both siblings that they did indeed have something of value. The inside of the box was quite elegant, even after apparent years of water submersion. The box was lined with a layer of metal, likely brass or bronze. There was a seal of some kind embossed into the metal lining the inside top of the box. It looked very official. Inside the box there was a pouch with drawstrings on one end. The drawstrings themselves looked to be made of leather, and looked still to be reasonably well preserved. The pouch also appeared to be leather, and it too had some type of seal on its side. Teagan and Jackson's eyes both got very large, and their mouths opened in awe. They looked at each other, and Teagan said, "Bro, I do indeed think we've found something!"

Jackson replied, "So it would appear. Certainly the inside of the box is impressive. Let's hope whatever is in the pouch is equally so. Just one way to find out. You do the honors."

Teagan grabbed the pouch in her left hand and then pulled the drawstrings with the fingers of her right hand.

"It feels heavy," she said, and then looked down into the pouch. "I don't see any coins in there. It looks like just one piece of something."

Still holding the outside of the pouch with her left hand she reached her thumb and forefinger into the pouch and grasped the object. She then slid it out of the pouch.

There was blinding light reflecting off the object. It was

near noon and the overhead sun light reflected so brightly as to make it difficult to look at their prize.

"Let's take it into the cabin .... the sun out here makes it impossible to examine," said Teagan.

The two then took their prize into the shaded cabin.

Teagan then held it out in her right hand and said, "I don't think I've ever seen anything as beautiful. It's obviously pure gold since there is absolutely no corrosion."

"It's gold okay," Jackson said as he rotated Teagan's right hand to get a good 360 degree look at the prize. "It's the shape of an anchor cross, and it has words inscribed on the horizontal arm of the cross."

"I do recall a little Latin," Teagan replied as she looked closely at the inscription. "Those words are **Pax Tecum**. They can be interpreted to mean 'Peace be with you'. What do you make of that?"

"Beats me," said Jackson as he continued to examine the artifact. "I'd say it's about six inches high, about four inches across, and maybe one-half inch thick. Pure gold. Just in today's gold market I bet the value of the gold alone would be over $100,000. But if I don't miss my guess, I bet it's worth a whole bunch more than that. Teagan, I think we've had a really, really good day!"

Teagan replied, "Oh yeah! I think we've struck the mother lode. Are you sure you didn't see any more of these things down there Jackson?"

Jackson laughed, and said, "Now don't get greedy. But seriously, no, I just saw the one faint blip that indicated this box. I didn't see anything else anywhere around."

Teagan replied, "Well, I think we should call it a day.....and WHAT a day!! But when we come back out, we'll continue where we left off today. If there are any more treasures like this anywhere around, we'll find them."

"We will indeed," said Jackson. "I agree to call it a day and head in. We need to get our prize to the Culture Ministry and let them do their thing to determine exactly what it is and what it's worth."

Teagan continued to hold and examine the anchor cross. She noticed that toward the top of the cross's vertical member there was a small hole that went completely through to the other side. She thought, 'That hole has to be there to permit it to be worn as a necklace'. She walked over to her cosmetic case and extracted a long, golden chain necklace and placed it through the hole in the artifact. Jackson then grabbed the two ends of the chain and fastened them around Teagan's neck. She was now wearing the anchor cross.

"Sister, I've got to tell you, stunning is just not sufficient to describe how you look wearing that anchor cross. Why don't you wear it all the way to the Culture Ministry's office. When they see it around your neck they'll have to increase their estimate of its worth by at least a million dollars!" Jackson said with a big smile.

Teagan beamed as she started the boat's engine and they headed toward the Ponza Harbor.

•••

After docking the boat in their reserved slip at the Ponza Harbor Marina, Teagan and Jackson secured the boat and then headed out of the marina. They walked across the floating walkway that linked the marina to the land, then through the parking lot, and finally they started walking up the steep ramp that led to the street where their office was located. This ramp was barely wide enough for one car, and had 10-feet-high concrete walls on each side. The ramp was about 50 yards long. When a car desired to go either up or down the ramp, the driver had to make sure no one was walking on the ramp and that no other cars were getting ready to enter from the opposite end.

"Climbing this ramp really uses the calories," Teagan said. "I bet I've lost five pounds since we've been here due to walking up this thing."

"Good exercise," said Jackson as they began the walk up the steep grade.

Unknown to them, a car had just cleared the top of the ramp, and the driver wanted to grab a soft drink from a machine that was located at the side of the roadway just beyond the ramp's top. He quickly put his car in park, opened his door, and jumped out and around the front of his car headed toward the soft-drink machine. Unfortunately, he only thought he put the car in park. In fact, in his haste, he had placed it in neutral. Although the grade was much less steep where he parked, it still had enough slope that the car started to slowly roll backward toward the steep ramp. The driver didn't notice it moving as he rushed to get his soft drink.

The siblings had gotten about half way up the ramp when they saw the car starting to roll down backwards. Jackson immediately looked toward the bottom of the ramp and realized that it was too far for them to make it before the car would hit them. The 10'-high concrete walls on each side made climbing out of the ramp impossible. The car was quickly gaining speed. There simply wasn't enough room on either side to avoid being run down by the runaway car. Teagan screamed. The siblings hugged as close as possible to one wall and Jackson tried to protect his sister by placing himself between her and the car, but they both knew they were goners.

And then the strangest thing happened. When the car was within just a few feet of them, it mysteriously veered quickly away from them and ran into the wall on the opposite side. It continued its downward journey scraping the wall across from the Langes. The car cleared Jackson and Teagan by just inches as it passed them, scraping the opposite wall.

"What was that all about," Jackson said as he started to breathe again.

"We're safe," whispered Teagan. "I don't know how or why, but we're safe."

Jackson continued to hug Teagan. He said, "That anchor cross you're wearing sure does feel hot. Do you feel it?"

"Now that you mention it, yes, it feels very warm," she replied.

"Just something else we don't understand," said Jackson

The siblings continued their assent of the ramp and then toward their office. A gentleman with a soft drink in his hand came running and screaming down the ramp toward the runaway car. The car finally came to a grinding halt at the bottom of the ramp....it's left side practically demolished.

•••

Teagan and Jackson arrived at their office. Teagan walked to one of their file cabinets and removed a set of the Culture Ministry forms which were used to officially register antiquities that were discovered in Italian waters. She sat at her desk and then completed the forms, describing the golden anchor cross they had discovered. Jackson then got their camera and took several photographs of their prize. He took pictures from all angles with the artifact sitting on the desk and then snapped a couple additional ones with Teagan wearing it as a necklace.

"Okay, Sis, you've got the forms and you're wearing our precious find. I've taken enough pictures of it. So I guess we're good to go to the Culture Ministry office to file our claim."

"I guess," replied a sad looking Teagan. "In the short time we've had the anchor cross I've really gotten attached to it. I just hate to have to give it up to the Culture Ministry." She was holding the artifact with her right hand and looking intently at it as it hung about her neck.

Jackson laughed and said, "I'll tell you one thing, it wouldn't do to go around wearing such a valuable necklace. I do think it rightly belongs in a museum. But you still have one more chance to enjoy wearing it to the office of the Culture Ministry. I'm sure Dr. Eden will welcome it with open arms."

The Ponza office of the Italian Culture Ministry (ICM) was located only about two blocks from the Siblings' TSP office. Dr. Verla Eden was the sole employee in Ponza's ICM office. Dr. Eden was a native of Naples, but was educated in the United States. She had received her doctorate in Archeological History from Georgetown University in Washington, D.C. She spoke English with just a hint of an accent and, of course, her native Italian. Verla was in her mid- forties, and was happily married to an American fisherman who had his own fishing business and boat here at the Ponza harbor. The two had married about 15 years ago and moved from Naples to Ponza.

"Oh, I'm sure it will be in good hands with Verla. I just hate to give it up. It is so beautiful," Teagan exclaimed.

"Okay, enough of that sentimental stuff," said Jackson. "I've got the papers; let's start walking to the ICM office. I'm really anxious to get Verla's take on what we have. I think if anyone would know, she would. We haven't stumped her yet with anything we brought her."

The siblings exited their TSP office, locked the door, and started the 10-minute walk to the ICM. There was a sidewalk just wide enough for two people. Teagan and Jackson walked side by side except when meeting another person. When that happened, Jackson fell behind his sister to allow room for the other person to pass. They had met a couple of people after about five minutes into their walk. Both had stared at the beautiful, golden anchor cross around Teagan's neck as they passed her.

Ninety-nine percent of the people that lived in Ponza were very peaceable, law abiding, and never got into trouble. Unfortunately for the Langes, they were getting ready to meet up with a person of the one percent that didn't fall into that category.

Jackson saw him coming. He looked to be maybe twenty years old, tall and skinny, with tattoos covering almost every inch of his visible skin. His pants were pulled down so low that about a foot of his red boxer shorts was on exhibit. He walked with sort of a sideways motion....probably necessary in order to keep his pants from falling off. His bald head had a baseball cap perched on it with the bill turned backwards. He was smoking something.....likely illegal. Trouble with a capital T.

Jackson fell behind Teagan to allow the person to pass. When he got almost beside Teagan he stuck out his right hand, grabbed the golden artifact, and started to pull it loose from Teagan's neck. He didn't hold it long! Immediately as the fingers of his right hand clutched the anchor cross a foul smelling smoke developed between the anchor cross and his hand. The man started screaming at the top of his lungs, released the artifact, and pulled his still smoking right hand back. He turned his palm toward his face to look at it. The skin had been burned so badly in several places that you could see what looked to be bone. Wisps of smoke were still evident. The man then turned and started to run in the direction from which he came. His pants fell to his ankles and he fell to the ground. He jumped up, jerked his pants up with his left hand, and started again to run with a loud string of foul words coming from his mouth.

Teagan and Jackson just stared in disbelief. Teagan then felt the heat from the anchor cross resting on her chest. It was now warm....but not hot. It felt just like it did earlier when the runaway car almost ran over them. Jackson touched it, smiled, nodded his head and said, "Sister, I don't understand any of this, but it would appear that this beautiful anchor cross has once again saved the day for us."

Teagan looked at her brother with a big smile and said, "Pax Tecum!"

They continued their walk to the Culture Ministry office.

• • •

"Buon giorno, Dr. Eden," Jackson said as he walked through the door at the office of the Culture Ministry with Teagan trailing behind him.

"Ciao, Jackson," replied Verla Eden. "Is that Teagan behind you?"

Teagan stepped from behind Jackson and said, "It is I, Dr. Eden. So good to see you!"

Verla took one look at Teagan and said, "What in the world is that gorgeous necklace you're wearing?"

Teagan and Jackson stood side by side at the counter. Verla Eden rose from her desk and walked to the counter to assist the siblings.

"Oh, you noticed it!" Teagan replied.

"I think I better find my sunglasses," said Verla. "I'm already about blinded from looking at it!"

"Isn't it adorable?" Teagan said. "I'd really like to keep it; but, I must confess, we found it on the sand bar this morning."

Jackson handed Verla the paperwork and said, "It was in this pouch, which was in this box." He placed them on the counter, then walked behind Teagan and reached up and unfastened her necklace. Teagan removed the chain and placed the anchor cross on the counter beside the pouch and box.

Verla carefully examined first the pouch, paying particular attention to the seal on its side. She then picked up the box and inspected it. She took several minutes looking at the embossed seal stamped in the interior metal lining. Finally, she focused on the anchor cross. She lifted it and turned it slowly 360 degrees. Then she looked carefully at all its sides. Then the color drained completely from her face.....she turned as white as snow. Her eyes got very large; her mouth opened without words. She reached behind and pulled up a stool to sit on.

Teagan and Jackson watched her carefully. Jackson said, "Are you okay, Dr. Eden? You don't look so good?"

Verla whispered, "No, no, I'm okay. It's just that after examining this anchor cross I suddenly realized what I think it is. And if I'm right, you folks have just located the Holy Grail of Roman antiquities!"

It was Teagan and Jackson's turn to feel faint! They looked

at each other with puzzled looks, and then each began to smile and nod their heads affirmatively.

Teagan said, "Dr. Eden, what exactly do you think it might be?"

Verla replied, "Well, I certainly can't be sure at this point, but all the indications seem to point to it being the Savior's Cross that belonged to Constantine the Great! The story goes that in 325 A.D. he responded to a vision by producing six beautiful, golden anchor crosses using gold given to him by Pope Sylvester I. The gold, called St. Peter's gold, was one bar of many that had been blessed by Jesus Christ and then given to Saint Peter to help start the church. In his vision Constantine saw a symbol that combined an anchor with a cross. He had accepted Christianity, and many historians think that in his vision he could have been thinking about two Bible verses. Hebrews 6:19 says, *'We have this hope* (meaning salvation through Christ) *as an anchor of the soul, sure and steadfast'*. And then First Corinthians 1:18 says, *'For the message of the cross is foolishness to those who are perishing, but to us who are being saved it is the power of God'.* He could have thought that in those two passages the Bible brought to light the significance of both the anchor and the cross, and those are symbolized together in the beautiful Savior's Crosses. Up until the time of Constantine the anchor was accepted by many as a religious symbol. It can be seen on gravestones dating back to well before the time of Christ. Constantine desired to make the cross the symbol of Christianity. From Christ's death on the cross until the time of Constantine, the cross was thought of in very negative terms because only the very worst criminals were put to death on crosses. Constantine changed all that."

"You say he made six of the Savior's Crosses?" asked Jackson.

"Yes, but he gave all but one to Pope Sylvester I. Constantine retained one for himself. And I'll have to do a little research to be certain of this, but I do believe that just recently all five of the Savior's Crosses given to the church have been accounted for. And that would leave only one remaining." Verla reached down, picked up the anchor cross, and said, "And this could just be it!"

Teagan said, "Wow, wow, and wow! Do you really think so?"

"We can certainly find out," Verla replied. "Give me a little time to make some contacts and I'll get back to you."

Jackson then said, "You should probably also be aware that in the short time we've had possession of the artifact it has twice demonstrated most unusual and mysterious power."

Verla said, "Oh, I'd love to know about those."

Jackson then went on to tell her about the incidents with the runaway car and with the attempted robbery.

Verla nodded her head in agreement as Jackson talked. She then said, "Those two incidents certainly fit well with the stories that surround the other five Savior's Crosses. Similar miraculous events are associated with each of them."

Verla continued, "I can also tell you that the seals on both the pouch and the box appear to be authentic Italian seals. They are of the type that were commonly in use during the second World War. Just the fact that they apparently are government seals and that the Constantine anchor cross was likely passed down through the Roman empire would also seem to go together. Why the seals appear to date to the period of WWII I don't know, but I will certainly check it out.

Teagan spoke, "Dr. Eden, you have demonstrated a remarkable knowledge. I know your love for history, particularly that associated with antiquities, but I'm still greatly impressed with your knowledge of the Savior's Crosses. Do you happen to know who could positively identify our artifact to establish that it is indeed Constantine's anchor cross?"

"You read my mind, Teagan," Verla replied. "And to answer your question, yes, I do think I know the name of a person who could prove its authenticity beyond any doubt."

"May we ask whom that might be?" asked Jackson.

"You certainly may," Verla replied. "There is a person at the University of Kentucky in the U.S. that I believe may currently have all five of the other anchor crosses. He is the director of a center there; I believe I recall it is called The Center for Appalachian Research, and he is THE authority on all the Constantine anchor crosses. If memory serves correctly, I believe his name is Dr. Peters. I will certainly be in contact with him. In addition, I'll do a little research with my own government to see what I can turn up about the seals on the pouch and box. Hopefully, that will help us to understand how the artifact came to be located on your sand bar."

Teagan then looked directly at Verla and said, "Dr. Eden, would you care to venture a guess as to the value of the Constantine anchor cross?"

Verla smiled, and said, "Honey, how do you place a value on the Holy Grail? If it is Constantine's anchor cross, it's absolutely unique. And its history is well known. But I know why you ask. You would like to know what reward you two could expect."

Jackson and Teagan both smiled really big and nodded affirmatively.

Verla continued, "Well, just let me say the number would undoubtedly be in the millions. I'd say well into the millions. But for the time being, just give me a little time to do some digging and I'll get back to you in a day or so."

"To say we'll be awaiting your call is somewhat of a gross understatement," Teagan said. "I don't know if we'll even be able to sleep until we hear back from you!"

"Sweet dreams and Pax Tecum," Verla said with a chuckle.

"Arriverderci," Teagan replied, and the siblings turned and walked out the door.

The moment the Langes departed her office, Dr. Eden, with shaking hands, picked up her telephone and called Dr. Alfonso Perilli, the Director of the Office of Culture Ministry's Antiquities Program in Naples.

"Buon giorno, Dr. Eden," said Dr. Perilli. "It's been a while. Good to hear your voice. I hope all is well on the beautiful isle of Ponza."

Verla replied, "Buon giorno to you, Dr. Perilli. Yes, thanks, things are fine here; but I just had something come into the office that I think might well be one of the most significant Italian antiquities discoveries of all times. I'm so nervous about it I can hardly hold the phone. I wanted to call to alert you and to see if I might get an appointment with you to bring it over for your inspection."

Dr. Alfonso Perilli was the ICM's foremost authority on antiquities. Verla had first met him when the two of them were graduate students at Georgetown University in Washington, D.C. Alfonso had received his undergraduate degree in history from Sapienza University in Rome and had taught high school history for five years before deciding to pursue an advanced degree. His love of history and antiquities drew him to begin a career with the ICM after receiving his doctorate degree. He quickly advanced up the ladder at the ICM and had been appointed the Director of its Antiquities Program about six years ago. Alfonso and Verla had maintained their friendship over the years, and Verla always sought Alfonso's advice on all matters related to Italian antiquities.

"Oh my," replied Dr. Perilli. "Now you've got my hand shaking. To hear you so excited over a find means to me that it very likely is genuine. I greatly respect your expertise and experience in such matters. Could you share a few of the details with me?"

Verla then described how the artifact came to her office and what she thought it might be. As she finished her explanation to Alfonso, her voice was so excited she could hardly speak.

"Verla, I'm astounded!" Dr. Perilli replied. "I can assure you I'll clear my calendar to see you and the artifact as soon as you might be able to get here." He thought a moment and then said, "Better still, how about I catch the first ferry out tomorrow morning and come to Ponza. I haven't visited your beautiful island in a while, and I would be just delighted to make the short journey. How about it?"

"That would be outstanding, Alfonso. The first ferry arrives at our harbor at 8:30 in the morning. I'll be at the dock to meet you. I have one question. Do you think I should invite the folks who found the Savior's Cross, the Langes, to our meeting?"

"That would be perfectly okay with me," he replied. "I know they must be about as excited as you are, and I would enjoy meeting them and sharing information with them."

"Super," replied Verla. "I'll call them just as soon as we finish our conversation, and I'll look forward greatly to seeing you first thing in the morning. Ciao, my friend."

"Ciao, Verla. See you at the dock at 8:30."

As soon as Verla hung up the phone from talking with Alfonso, she dialed the Langes and invited them to the meeting with Dr. Perilli. They quickly agreed and said they would meet her in the morning at the ferry dock at 8:30. She then walked to a filing cabinet and pulled out a thick file marked "Savior's Crosses Info". She took the file back to her desk, sat, and opened it. She thumbed through numerous newspaper articles until she found the information she was looking for. She then reached again for her phone and started dialing.

●●●

Dr. Randy Peters is Director of the University of Kentucky's Center for Appalachian Research (CAR), a position he has held now for some 23 years. He is the first and only Director of the CAR. For his first eight years things had gone well, but largely just academic, compiling useful information about Kentucky's beautiful Appalachian mountain region. Randy had a special interest in Harlan County, located in the extreme Southeastern portion of the state. While at the University of Virginia he had written his Doctoral dissertation addressing the history and development of Harlan County. And then, about 15 years ago, something happened in Harlan County that completely changed Dr. Peters' focus at the CAR. A 10-year-old boy, named Kylie Potter, was exploring in the woods and happened across the decaying ruins of the wagon that belonged to Reverend Karl and Mary Seibert, early pioneers who were killed by Indians while in route to Harlan in 1798. Kylie discovered among the ruins a beautiful, golden anchor cross that Dr. Peters' research revealed was one of Constantine Savior's Crosses. The Seibert Anchor Cross was then responsible for preventing the death of several people during an attempted bank robbery in Harlan. Three and a half million dollars of illegal drug money was discovered in lock boxes during the botched robbery. The money was subsequently divided between three entities: (1) Kylie Potter in a trust fund, (2) Harlan County to establish The Seibert Anchor Cross Memorial building on the grounds of the Harlan County Court House, and (3) to the CAR to establish an anchor cross research program to allow Dr. Peters to further investigate the history and location of all six Savior's Crosses.

Twelve years passed before the second of the Savior's Crosses was located. It was discovered in a church in Prato, Italy.   Mr. Domenico Pelle, owner of Italy's famed Pelle vineyards and winery, had placed the artifact to be displayed in the church. It had been passed down through his family for generations after having been given to his great, great grandfather by Pope Pius IX. Domenico Pelle agreed to let Dr. Peters take his anchor cross to the CAR for the purpose of establishing its authenticity. By comparing microscopic surface analysis between the Seibert and Pelle anchor crosses, Randy was able to confirm that the two were cast in the same mold. Further assurance was established when tiny bits of gold were scraped from the two artifacts and analyzed to establish that the gold from each anchor cross was identical.

The Helena Anchor Cross, the third to be located, was found about a year later when Harlan Pastor Raymond Bell was on a mission trip to the Seychelles and discovered the anchor cross in a chapel on a plantation owned by a Mr. Felix Faure. It too was authenticated by Dr. Peters at the CAR. Randy's research revealed that it had been taken to Jerusalem by Constantine's mother, Helena, in 326 A.D. and had been stolen from there in 1860 by thieves. It was then aboard an ill-fated ship that went down in a violent storm off the Seychelles. Two survivors on a raft washed ashore on the Faure plantation. One of the two was wearing the Helena Anchor Cross.

Amazingly, about a year after the Helena Anchor Cross was found, two twin sisters in the lineage of the French King Louis XV heard about the discoveries of the other three

Savior's Crosses from the coverage by the world media, and decided to reveal their stories about the final two Savior's Crosses that Constantine gave to Pope Sylvester I. The Carmen Sisters invited Renee Dubois, a reporter for the Paris based newspaper *Le Monde*, to write their stories. Mademoiselle Dubois had written extensively about the discoveries of the three previous anchor crosses and contacted Dr. Peters to ask him to authenticate the two claimed by the Carmen sisters. After testing, they were determined indeed to be genuine.

Thus, Dr. Randy Peters currently had all five of the anchor crosses given by Constantine to Pope Sylvester I in his center at the University of Kentucky. All owners of the artifacts had agreed to allow Randy to keep them for a period at the CAR for study and research. His center had received great international publicity from all the world-wide media coverage of the beautiful, golden anchor crosses and the stories associated with them.

Randy's secretary, Joyce, buzzed him on his intercom and said, "Dr. Peters, there's a Dr. Verla Eden calling you from Italy. She says she needs to talk with you regarding the Constantine Anchor Cross. Would you want to talk with her?"

Seated at his desk, Randy got a very inquisitive look on his face and said, "Does this Dr. Eden sound like a nutcase, or does she sound legit?"

"She sounds okay," Joyce replied. "But as you know, it's really hard to tell."

"Okay Joyce, I'll talk with her. If she proves to be a nutcase, I'm going to dock your pay," Randy joked.

"This is Dr. Randy Peters, Dr. Eden, I understand you wish to chat about the Constantine Anchor Cross."

"Yes, Dr. Peters, I do. As a matter of fact, I think I currently have it in my possession!"

Randy was starting to think about docking Joyce's pay as he said, "And where, may I ask, did you locate it?"

Verla continued to tell Randy the story behind her having the anchor cross. When she finished, she said, "I know you likely think me less than creditable, but let me assure you the story I have just told you is true. I operate Italy's Office of Culture Ministry on the island of Ponza, off Italy's Western coast. My superior, Dr. Alfonso Perilli, the Director of the Office of Culture Ministry's Antiquities Program in Naples, has been advised of this discovery and is coming to Ponza tomorrow morning to examine the artifact. My reason for contacting you is twofold, namely (1) I wanted to alert you about the artifact, and (2) I wanted to know if it would be possible to have you examine it to establish its authenticity. I am aware that you are the foremost authority on these artifacts, and that your center currently has the other five. I do have photographs and could email them to you, and I could also share Dr. Perilli's thoughts after his examination tomorrow."

Randy was struggling to hold the telephone. His mouth had dropped open and his free hand had hit his coffee cup, spilling coffee on his desk. Most of the color had drained from his face. He tried to reply, "Dr. Eden, if what you say proves to be true, I would be more than willing to do anything you would ask of me. Constantine's Anchor Cross, as I'm sure you know, is not only the last of the six that he cast, but it was his personal anchor cross. The other five he gave to the Pope. I've been trying for many, many years to locate it. Could you please send me the pictures you have of it. That would really help me."

Verla said, "Certainly. I can do that right away....I've already scanned them to my computer. If you would give me your email address I could send them as we talk."

Randy gave her his email address and then about lost consciousness when the images appeared on his computer screen.

Randy said, "Dr. Eden, those are either the best forgeries I've ever seen or they are indeed the Constantine Anchor Cross! I'll be extremely anxiously awaiting to hear from you tomorrow after you get Dr. Perilli's assessment."

"I think I can detect that you are as excited about this as I am," replied Verla. "I'll report our phone conversation to Alfonso and then get right back to you with his comments after he's had the chance to examine it. Thank you so very much for listening to me; and if I don't miss my guess, I think we will be seeing each other before long."

"I think you are correct," Randy replied. "I thank you for contacting me, and I'll look forward greatly to your phone call tomorrow. Arriverderci, my new friend."

"Ciao," replied Verla.

•••

Verla was standing on the dock at the Ponza Harbor Marina at 8:20 am. She was staring in the direction from which she knew the ferry would be approaching. Her mind was racing....thinking about all of yesterday's events.

"Buon giorno!" The greeting caused Verla to jump. She turned to see the Langes approaching.

"Buon giorno to you, my friends," Verla replied. "I was standing here deep in thought, and your voice startled me."

"Sorry 'bout that," replied Jackson. "Teagan always said I was a loud mouth!"

"Oh no, my friend, that you are not!" Verla said. "Hey, I see the ferry approaching. I do hope Alfonso made it aboard!"

"We'll see soon enough!" replied Teagan.

Verla, Teagan, and Jackson walked to, and stood beside, the slip where the ferry would dock. As the ferry was coming into its slip, they saw Dr. Perilli standing on the ferry deck waving at them. As soon as the dock lines were secured and the gangway was in place, Dr. Perilli came trotting off the boat with a big smile.

As he approached the three he greeted, "Buon giorno!"

Verla replied, "Buon giorno, Dr. Perilli, it is so good to see you made it. I would like to introduce my friends, Teagan and Jackson Lange. They operate a dive company here called Thomas Salvaging Ponza and yesterday found the artifact that has us all so excited."

Dr. Perilli vigorously shook hands with the Langes and gave a big hug to Verla, then said, "I'm so pleased to meet you. Verla has told me about your find and has sent me pictures of the treasure. I'm very anxious to examine it and hope it proves to be what we all think it might be."

The foursome continued to chat as they walked back to Verla's ICM office.

Once at the office, Verla pulled up chairs around her desk for everyone. She then walked to the wall safe and after dialing the combination, opened it and extracted the box containing the golden anchor cross which had been placed back in its pouch. She carried the box to her desk, placed it down, and took her seat. She then turned the box such that its hinged lid opened on the side facing her visitors. She slowly opened it.

Immediately visible was the ornate inside lining of the box with the embossed seal. The pouch had been placed such that the seal on its side was also visible.

Dr. Perilli took one good look at the seals and said, "Before we open the pouch, I already can tell you what I believe will be important information. The seals I see on both the inside lid and on the pouch are very special. They were only used for a short period of time and were used by only one person. The person was Prime Minister Benito Mussolini, and the period during which he utilized the seals was in 1943. If you will permit me, let me digress a little to put this in historical perspective. You may already know all this - I'm sure Verla does; but Mussolini formed the National Fascist Party and ruled Italy as Prime Minister from 1922 until his ousting in 1943. He ruled from 1922 until 1925 under the existing constitution but then dropped all pretense of democracy and set up a legal dictatorship known as Il Duce. He was the founder of fascism. He remained in power until being deposed by King Victor Emmanuel III in 1943. By the middle of 1943 things were certainly not going well for Mussolini, and on July 24, 1943, soon after the start of the Allied invasion of Italy, the Grand Council of Fascism voted against him, and King Emmanuel had him arrested the following day. Guards took him on July 28 aboard a fast-moving naval vessel to the island of Ponza. He was imprisoned right here on this island until August 7th, at which time he was moved to the island of La Maddalena off Sardinia. He later escaped and went to northern Italy but was quickly captured and executed near Lake Como by Italian partisans. His body was taken to Milan where it hung upside down for public viewing. Enough of the history lesson, now back to the seals. For whatever reason, Mussolini commissioned the seals you see here inside this box for use only on his personal papers and items. The seals started to appear sometime in early 1943. Many of his papers that are dated January to July, 1943 appear with the seal. Also, there are numerous of his personal items, things like jewelry, vases, brief cases, etc. that bear the seal and are now in Italian museums. So, the fact that this treasure bears these seals is certainly indicative that what is inside the pouch was the personal possession of Prime Minister Benito Mussolini!"

"Wow, wow and wow!" Teagan replied. "That's fascinating and amazing."

"It is, indeed," replied Verla. "But what could explain how the box came to be located on the sand bar?"

"Well," said Alfonso, "Here's the rest of the story. It is known that after the Prime Minister was arrested by the King, he was quickly taken to Ponza. For reasons unknown, he was allowed to gather a number of his personal belongings, and they were shipped separately to Ponza. I guess his belongings were more than the naval boat carrying him could, or wanted, to accommodate. So, a few days after Mussolini arrived on Ponza, the ferry carrying his belongings was hit with a sudden very strong storm that sank it. Debris from the wreckage was later found over a large area, being driven by the storm waters. Some of Mussolini's personal items were discovered. It would be my guess that this box was tight enough to allow it to float free of the wreckage and then drifted in the waters until it finally sank to the sand bar where you found it yesterday. That's just speculation, of course, but it certainly could have happened that way."

Jackson said, "That is one interesting story, Dr. Perilli, and I think your speculation about the box likely explains how it came to be on the sand bar."

"Okay, my friends, I think the time has come to take a look inside the pouch," Dr. Perilli exclaimed. He grasped it, opened the draw strings, and then pulled out the anchor cross. It's brilliance lit up the room almost like a light bulb. "It is absolutely stunning. Truly, I've never, ever seen anything to compare to it. Without running any tests, I can tell you that I believe it is certainly genuine. I don't think something this beautiful could possibly be faked. But, I guess we do need to cover all our bases and try and get analyses that establish beyond any doubt that it is Constantine's anchor cross. I know you three have discussed the history surrounding the Savior's crosses, so I won't repeat that. Just let me say that if this does in fact prove to be the one that Constantine kept for himself, it will rank as perhaps the most significant antiquity find of the modern era."

"So, you think it might be worth some bucks," Teagan joked.

"Yes, my dear, I think it would be safe to say that," replied Dr. Perilli.

Dr. Eden then asked, "If it is the real deal, would you care to venture a guess as to it's value?"

"No," replied Dr. Perilli. "Being unique and given its history, I really couldn't even make a guess right now. But I can certainly say that in U.S. dollars it would be worth many, many millions. How many, I just don't know."

Jackson started rubbing his hands together. Jackson and Teagan got huge smiles on their faces.

Verla then said, "Okay, so I think we should now put in motion the process to authenticate it. And the only way I know to do that is to call Dr. Randy Peters, tell him what we think, and see if he'd be willing to become involved and perform the necessary testing to establish our artifact as being Constantine's anchor cross. Do you agree?"

Teagan and Jackson nodded vigorously. Dr. Perilli said, "I do agree, Verla. Why don't you give him a call."

"I would be happy to," she said, "but I don't think he would be in his office. In the U.S. it's only about 4 a.m.! Could I suggest we go to an early lunch. We can continue to discuss our thoughts about the anchor cross and then come back to the office this afternoon and give Dr. Peters a call."

All three nodded approvingly, and they left for lunch.

•••

Dr. Peters normally arrived at his office around 7 a.m., well before the rest of his employees, including his secretary, Joyce. This morning he had arrived a bit earlier than normal. He hadn't slept well, due largely to the phone call he had received yesterday from Dr. Eden saying she thought she had Constantine's anchor cross in her possession. Randy had made coffee and had just poured a cup and was sitting at his desk when his phone rang. He normally would just let it ring....he got so many nutcases calling about the anchor crosses; but because he was expecting a call from Dr. Eden, and because he realized that because of the time difference it was now afternoon in Italy, he picked up the phone. "Hello. This is Dr. Randy Peters."

"Buon giorno Dr. Peters, this is Dr. Verla Eden. You are an early bird; I didn't know if you'd be in your office this early, but thought I'd take a chance on catching you."

"Buon giorno to you, Dr. Eden. With the news you gave me yesterday I had a hard time sleeping last night, so I just got up early and came in to work. I'm so glad you called, and I'm all ears to hear what you've discovered."

"Thank you, Dr. Peters," Verla replied. "Let me tell you that I've got Dr. Alfonso Perilli and Teagan and Jackson Lange here in my office with me. I'll put my phone on 'speaker'. We've all spent the morning examining the artifact, and I'll let Dr. Perilli speak for himself."

"Dr. Perilli, it's so good to be able to speak to you. I've heard great things about you from Dr. Eden," Randy said.

Dr. Perilli replied, "The pleasure is all mine, Dr. Peters. I truly feel like I already know you through all the articles I've read of your investigations regarding the Savior's crosses. If you'll permit me, I'll come right to the point. The beautiful, golden artifact that is positioned before me as we speak is, in my opinion, that molded by Constantine the Great and kept as his personal anchor cross. I say this based solely on its appearance, and my close examination of it. I know that we require your laboratory examination and comparison to the other Savior's crosses before its authenticity can be fully established, and it would be my recommendation that you proceed to do exactly that."

Randy said, "Dr. Perilli, your words are like music to my ears! I've been searching for many years to try and locate the Constantine anchor cross, and now based upon what you and Dr. Eden have told me, and the photographs she sent me, my guess is that the search is over. I'm excited beyond description. Do you have any idea how the artifact came to be located on the sand bar?"

Alfonso then gave a short version of the Mussolini story to Randy.

"Amazing, just astounding!" said Randy. "So I guess Constantine's anchor cross did somehow stay in the Italian government from 325 to 1943. That in itself is truly remarkable. And then it gets taken by Mussolini and lost in a sunken ferryboat, and again discovered yesterday on the sandbar by the Langes. What a fantastic story."

"It is," Verla said. "So what's the next step?"

Randy said, "From all the information you folks have given me, I really don't see any reason why I would need to come to Ponza. The tests to authenticate the artifact must be made here in Lexington at my center. Do you think it would be possible for any or all of you to bring it to Lexington?"

Teagan and Jackson nodded their heads and then Jackson said, "Dr. Peters, this is Jackson Lange speaking. My sister Teagan and I certainly could do that, and it would be super if Drs. Eden and Perilli could come as well."

Dr. Perilli then said with a smile, "I don't think four people would be required to transport it! Verla and I will stay here, but will keep in contact and anxiously await hearing from you. Technically, since the artifact now officially belongs to Italy, we'll have to fill out some paperwork to permit the Langes to travel with it, but that's just a formality. Let me also say that I certainly look forward to meeting you personally in the near future, and I know I speak for Verla also."

Verla said, "Indeed you do, Alfonso. And we deeply thank you for all your assistance with this, Dr. Peters."

"A genuine pleasure," Randy replied. "Please give all my contact information to Teagan and Jackson, and I'll look forward to hearing back from them after they make their travel arrangements. Arriverderci, my friends."

After hanging up the phone, Verla looked at the three sitting across her desk and gave a big 'thumbs up'. Dr. Perilli then said, "Friends, I think we should call it a most successful day and go out together to celebrate!"

"Absolutely," said Teagan and Jackson in unison, and after Verla replaced the Constantine anchor cross in her safe the friends left the ICM office for a bit of celebrating.

•••

Jackson and Teagan arrived at their villa around 6 p.m. They had enjoyed celebrating with the ICM folks. It was certainly a day to remember.

Teagan said, "I know it's about noon in the U.S. Maybe we can catch all the Thomases at lunch. I think we should call and give them the news!"

Jackson replied, "Yeah, probably should, even though it's still not 100% until Dr. Peters' evaluation. But I agree, we should make the call."

Teagan grabbed the phone and placed the call.

"I hope this call doesn't mean bad news from Ponza!" answered Cooper Thomas.

"Well, and a buon giorno to you, too," Teagan replied. "And actually, no, as a matter of fact, I think we're getting ready to share the best news you could possibly expect. And if Clayton and Lillie are there with you please put your phone on 'speaker', and I'll do the same on this end. Then everyone can hear and speak."

"Boy, sounds important!" said Cooper. "Clayton and Lillie are right here. You caught us in the office getting ready to wolf sandwiches. Okay, everyone's hearing you on this end. We're ready for some really good news!"

Jackson then started the story, beginning with their find on the sand bar, the experiences they had with the runaway car on the ramp and the nutcase that tried to steal the anchor cross, and finally with all that had happened with the ICM folks and the response from Dr. Peters.

When finished, there was a long pause on the other end of the phone, and Jackson finally said, "You folks still there?"

Lillie spoke, "Oh yes, yes indeed we're here. We're just about speechless."

"If we understood everything correctly," Clayton said, "it sounds as though the Holy Grail showed up at Ponza! And you found it! Astounding.....beyond words."

"We need to still be a little cautious," replied Teagan. "Until Dr. Peters makes it official, we've only discovered a golden artifact worth around $100,000 in gold. If he does establish it as the Constantine anchor cross, then I think we could all retire!"

"I agree," said Lillie. "We shouldn't count our chickens before they hatch, but from everything I hear from you it certainly does sound encouraging. Do you think Dr. Peters would mind if the three of us came up to Lexington to be with you when you take him the prize?"

"I can't see any reason he would object.....and after all, we're all in this together!" replied Jackson. "We'll get on the web tonight and start looking for suitable flights to Lexington; and when we've got them, we'll get back with you guys, and you can make your arrangements. That sound okay?"

"Perfect," said Lillie. "Now we here in Key West may all spend the rest of the day and night counting our chickens!" Lillie chuckled, and then continued, "But seriously, we are pleased beyond description with what you two have accomplished. Our faith in you is rewarded beyond measure! We'll be looking to hear from you as soon as you have your travel arrangements completed. Take care."

"Arriverderci," said Teagan as she disconnected her phone. She then walked to her computer and started searching for plane tickets.

Chapter 2

Lexington, Kentucky

The Langes and the Thomases had gotten adjoining two-bedroom suites at the Lexington Hyatt. Teagan and Jackson Lange each had a bedroom in one suite, and Lillie Thomas had a private bedroom in the other suite while her brothers Cooper and Clayton shared one. The door between the two suites was open, and the good friends had all gathered in the Lange's suite. Everyone was seated around a small table. The center of attention was the spectacular necklace being worn by Teagan. She had previously shown it to all the Thomases, allowing each of them to carefully inspect it. Never had there been so many oohs and ahhs uttered in a room at the Hyatt. All of the Thomases agreed that the golden anchor cross was the most beautiful artifact they had ever seen. Everyone now continued to stare at it as it hung from Teagan's neck.

"I feel funny with all you looking at me," Teagan said. "But I understand, it really is something, isn't it?"

Lillie replied, "You can say that again! It really is something! Ole Constantine certainly did good work."

Cooper said, "Yeah, but to believe that you guys were lucky enough to find it is what I find incredible. The odds against that were almost beyond measure."

"True enough," said Jackson. "We did certainly get very lucky. But you guys were the ones that placed us in that part of the world to look for treasure. So we all should take a lot of pride in being a vital part of this find. Sometimes things just work out, and boy did they ever here."

"I don't want to sound negative," said Clayton, "but we still don't know 100% for sure that this is Constantine's anchor cross. Maybe we should hold off on all the big celebration until Dr. Peters has confirmed our find."

Lillie replied, "Clayton has a point. The good news is that we won't have to wait long. Our appointment with him is tomorrow morning.....maybe we can plan a big celebration tomorrow evening."

They all nodded in agreement, and continued to stare at the golden anchor cross.

• • •

The following morning Randy Peters arrived at his office at 6:30 a.m., about a half hour earlier than normal for him. His excitement had prevented him from a good night's sleep, and he finally got up early and headed for the office. It was just hard for him to believe that in just a couple of hours the Constantine anchor cross would enter his office. He had been searching for it for so many years, and had been totally unsuccessful. Then he got the phone call from Dr. Eden, and everything changed. The last of the Savior's Crosses had been discovered! At least he hoped so. But every indication pointed to it's being the real deal. In just a short time now he'd hopefully be able to establish its authenticity. Boy oh boy, was he excited. He got up from his desk and got another cup of coffee. This was going to be a really long two hours.

At about 5 minutes before 9 a.m. the voice of Randy's secretary, Joyce, was heard on his intercom saying, "Dr. Peters, you have visitors.....the Langes and the Thomases."

"By all means please show them in," replied Randy as he almost tipped over his coffee cup.

The door to his office opened and in paraded five young folks.....all with huge smiles on their faces. Their hands were immediately extended to Randy, and after firmly shaking hands with each of them he said, "Please, please, have a seat. We have a lot to talk about!"

Pleasantries were exchanged, and after a few moments of chit-chat Randy just couldn't wait any longer and said, "I really don't want to seem too anxious.....but I am! Would you mind if I could now have a look at the anchor cross?"

Teagan was wearing a button-up sweater over a white blouse. She reached under the sweater and pulled out the golden artifact. She then removed it from around her neck, and handed it across the desk to Randy.

Randy's hands were shaking so much he didn't know if he would be able to keep from dropping it. He finally placed it on his desk. His eyes got very large, and his mouth opened in awe as he carefully examined it. In his mind there was no doubt about it ..... this was Constantine's anchor cross.

"I know it's a trite expression, but words just cannot express the beauty and magnificence of this artifact," Randy declared. "And not only just its physical appearance, but to know that this anchor cross lying on my desk is made from pure gold that was once blessed by our Lord Jesus Christ and then given to Saint Peter to help start the church, and then, some 325 years later, cast by Roman Emperor Constantine the Great into this form, and was possessed by him for the remainder of his life ..... just beyond comprehension!"

"So I take it you think it might be genuine?" Lillie asked.

Randy laughed and replied, "I would bet the farm on it. But we'll know for absolute certain in just a few hours. With your permission I'll pass it to my staff to perform the necessary tests to establish its authenticity."

All nodded in agreement, and then Cooper said, "I think that's what we're here for."

Randy then gathered the anchor cross, stood, and said, "If you'll excuse me for just a few minutes I'll personally take it to the lab and see that testing gets underway immediately. Please help yourself to the coffee, and I believe there might be some cookies there in the tray beside the urn. I'll return shortly."

As Randy left his office, the five guests nodded and smiled in agreement, and then lined up for refreshments.

•••

Randy returned to his office after about ten minutes. His five visitors were all talking with each other and enjoying their refreshments. Randy said, "Sorry to leave you, but I think we've got everything on track to have the testing finished on the anchor cross by early afternoon. If it suits everyone I thought we could take a little tour of my lab and see the other five anchor crosses, and then head over to the faculty club for lunch. I have the President's Room reserved for us. I think you'll enjoy it. After lunch we can come back here and hopefully get the good news about the Constantine anchor cross. That sound okay with everyone?"

"Sounds real good, Randy," offered Jackson. "I know we all would like to see the other anchor crosses, and the luncheon sounds great." The other four visitors nodded in agreement, and everyone stood and followed Randy out of his office headed for the lab.

•••

"That lunch was superb," said Lillie. "First time I've ever had a Kentucky Hot Brown....it sure was a treat."

"Yeah," said Randy, "they do a good job on those. If you like turkey, ham , and cheese you can't beat a Hot Brown, and it is a native dish.....named for the Brown Hotel in Louisville, where they were first served."

Randy and his visitors had assembled back in his office after having lunch. Randy was passing out peppermints to everyone when his intercom sounded, "Dr. Peters, Rod Bird is here to see you."

Randy nodded to everyone and said, "This is the news we've been waiting for!"

He then said to Joyce on his intercom, "By all means please send Rod in."

The office door opened, and in walked Randy's chief lab technician, Rod Bird.

Rod had the anchor cross in one hand, a report in his other hand, and a big smile on his face. Randy introduced him to the visitors, and then said, "From the size of that smile I'd say you might have some good news for us."

"I could never fool you, boss," Rod replied. "And you guessed it, the news is very good." Rod handed the report to Randy and carefully placed the artifact on Randy's desk. "After running all the required tests, we are 100% certain that this is the 6th Constantine anchor cross."

The visitors all stood and started slapping each other on their backs, shaking hands, and congratulating everyone. Rod Bird then turned and left the office. Randy and his guests all took their seats. Everyone just stared at the golden anchor cross.

"Well, that's the good news we were hoping for," said Randy. "You did indeed find Constantine's anchor cross. Of course you are free to take it with you, but if you would rather I can certainly keep it here in the Center for safe keeping..... that's entirely up to you. But you do need to understand that the value of this artifact is absolutely priceless."

"We do understand that," replied Teagan. "I, for one, would vote to let you keep it here. I think it would be much safer." The other four nodded in agreement.

"I'll be happy to," Randy replied. "Now, we need to talk about a news conference. Currently no one other than us, the folks here in my center, and Dr. Eden and Dr. Perilli are aware of your discovery. This news is so important, we certainly wouldn't want it to get accidently leaked to the press. It would be far better to take the bull by the horns, so to speak, and schedule a news conference to make sure that only correct information gets passed to the media. Do you think we could schedule one for tomorrow morning?"

The five guests looked at each other, then Cooper spoke up, "That sounds fine to me. The five of us can have our little celebration party tonight, and then disclose the Constantine anchor cross to the world tomorrow. What time would you suggest?"

Randy replied, "Well, if we schedule it for 10 a.m. that will give them time to have it on television for the noon news, and would be plenty of time for the print media to get their stories in to be published the following day. Radio will go with the news almost as soon as the news conference concludes. Would 10 a.m. suit you guys?"

Each of the five looked at the others, then Teagan said, "10 a.m. it is. We really appreciate so much your help and hospitality, Dr. Peters."

"Believe me, it's my pleasure. You just can't know how happy I am that you brought this marvelous artifact to my attention. I feel like a good part of my life's work has just concluded!" Randy replied. "I would suggest you might next wish to make a phone call to Dr. Eden to let her know the news, and she could then call Dr. Perilli."

"Good thinking," Teagan replied. The group continued to chat for another fifteen minutes, then the guests left and Randy collected the anchor cross and took it to the lab where it would be placed in a display case along with the other five.

●●●

The Next Morning

The Center for Appalachian Research had a large conference room. It had served on many occasions as a site for news conferences. It was now about 9:45 a.m., and the media had been arriving for the past hour. A large table had been arranged at the front of the room, with six chairs behind it. The Langes and Thomases were already seated. Randy was walking around the room greeting each of the media representatives as they arrived. Radio and television stations from Cincinnati, Louisville, Knoxville, and Lexington were represented. Newspaper personnel from each of these cities as well as many smaller towns in Kentucky were seated. All of the major networks had representatives. Randy stopped to chat for a moment with his good friend Barbara Clark from Lexington's CBS affiliate, channel 27 television. Barbara was a native of Harlan, and had been an anchor for WKYT for many years.

Barbara looked at her watch and said, "Almost 10 o'clock....it's about show time!"

Randy grinned and replied, "It is indeed. I'll head back up front." He walked back behind the front table and took a seat beside his five guests. He reached for the microphone sitting on the table before him.

"Good morning ladies and gentlemen of the press. For the record, I'm Dr. Randy Peters, Director of UK's Center for Appalachian Research, or CAR. My guess would be that each of you has been to a news conference here at the CAR previously, and most likely it was to cover a story related to the anchor crosses. Today represents the grand finale. I'm so very pleased to report that the sixth and final anchor cross has been discovered, and we will display it for you in just a moment. Before that, I would like to introduce the people sitting here with me. On my right and your left are the Thomases. On the end is Clayton, in the middle is Cooper, and this lovely lady on my right is Lillie Thomas. They are the principals in the firm of Thomas Salvaging, LLC, in Key West, Florida. The couple on my left and your right are the Langes; Jackson on the end, and his sister Teagan here next to me on my left. The Langes operate Thomas Salvaging Ponza, or TSP, located on the island of Ponza, off the Western coast of Italy. TSP is owned by the Thomases; the Langes are partners with the Thomases in that operation. All of these folks are involved in recovering sunken treasure from the sea. Just about a week ago Jackson was diving on a sand bar located close to Ponza, and Teagan was operating their dive boat. They happened upon a very unusual box buried in the sand bar, and inside the box was found the holy grail of antiquities, the Constantine Anchor Cross. This artifact was reported as required by law to the Italian authorities, who are the current owner, but they gave their permission to the Langes to bring it here to the CAR to have a series of tests performed on it to determine its authenticity. Those tests were completed yesterday afternoon, and they showed conclusively that the artifact is indeed Constantine's anchor cross."

Randy then nodded to Teagan. She reached down and removed the cloth that was covering the golden anchor cross. She then grasped it, and held it vertically for all to see. Gasps were heard throughout the room. Other than those, the only sounds to be heard were the motors of the video cameras rolling in the back of the room and the clicking of the shutters on the still cameras, the flashes from which made the room into a virtual lightning storm. Teagan rotated the artifact 360 degrees, and then moved it slowly from left to right. The photography session lasted for another five minutes.

Randy then stood and said, "We'll now be happy to take questions." The questions began and lasted for another 30 minutes. During that time they were asked about the box containing the anchor cross. Its history as related by Dr. Perilli was told to them. There were many questions about ownership, and these were expertly fielded by several of the treasure hunters. There were questions about the value of the anchor cross, and Jackson told them that it was absolutely priceless; that no value had been set for it. Barbara Clark, with CBS affiliate WKYT in Lexington, asked whether the Langes had occasion to experience with the Constantine anchor cross the supernatural power associated with all the previous five anchor crosses. Teagan then related the story about how she and Jackson were saved from the runaway car coming down the ramp when Teagan was wearing the anchor cross, and then Jackson told the story of the punk who tried to jerk the anchor cross from Teagan as they walked to Dr. Eden's office.

At the conclusion of the questions the media were invited to come up to the head table to get close looks at the artifact, and to take additional pictures if desired. Although some rushed out of the conference room to call in their stories, several did take advantage of the additional time to see and photograph the magnificent golden anchor cross. After another 15 or so minutes the media had all left to file their stories. Only Randy and his five guests were left at the head table.

"Well, as I now speak the stories are flooding out to all corners of the Earth about the discovery of the Constantine anchor cross," Randy said to the five. "I thought everything went very well, and I really appreciate your help very much."

Cooper Thomas replied, "I'm sure I can speak for all of us in saying how thankful we are for your expert assistance. I spoke with both Dr. Eden and Dr. Perilli, and they both agreed that we should leave the anchor cross with you for the time being. They felt it would be safer, and that you could possibly use it in some of your research. They also said that they both wanted to come to Lexington in the not too distant future to meet you and to discuss the future of the Constantine anchor cross."

"Outstanding," Randy replied. "I know you all have plane reservations for flying back home this afternoon, so why don't I suggest we have lunch again at the faculty club, and then I'll drive you to the airport in our van."

"Sounds like a plan to me," said Clayton. Randy gathered the anchor cross and they all followed him out of the conference room. It had been a great day!

Chapter 3

❦

About a month earlier
Pyongyang, North Korea

Kim Jong-un, the 32-year-old 3rd Supreme Leader of North Korea, sat at his desk in one of his many palaces reading reports. It was a job he didn't like, but had learned from experience that it was one even the Supreme Leader really should do. He would much rather be watching a basketball game, having someone executed, or eating. Just the thought of eating brought on pain from his gout. At 5'5" tall and 330 pounds, Kim's gout had continued to grow worse. Perhaps he should have his personal trainer executed.

He then came to a report that about a month ago he had requested be prepared. Kim had noticed stories reported on the international media about some kind of strange golden artifacts that seemed to have very unusual and strong powers to protect those who possessed them. He had requested his research team to investigate fully the stories and prepare a report that contained their findings. He eagerly read the report.

He then sat back in his chair, placed his gout-plagued feet on his desk, and reflected on the contents of the report. If he correctly understood what it said, a total of five of the golden artifacts had been found; they were called Savior's crosses or anchor crosses and were located at a university in the U.S. Apparently they had been made by Roman Emperor Constantine the Great in 325 A.D. What really fascinated Kim was that each of these anchor crosses seemed to be capable of protecting the person wearing it. There were many such stories contained in the report. From reading these, he gathered that anyone wearing one could do virtually anything without possibility of harm. If that was true, he wanted to have them. Think what could be done! Persons each wearing one of the Savior's crosses could go anywhere and do anything without being stopped. Kim continued to dream they could even walk into the White House and grab the President of the United States! Demands could then be made that would have to be granted. He could rule the world! All he needed was to get his hands on those five anchor crosses.

He sat up and punched a button on his intercom.

"Yes, Supreme Leader, what is your wish?" came the voice on the other end.

"My demand is that a meeting be scheduled for tomorrow at 1 p.m. I want to meet with the authors of the report titled 'The Anchor Crosses'."

"Yes, Supreme Leader, it shall be scheduled."

•••

Kim Jong-un is the youngest son of Kim Jong-il, the second Supreme Leader of North Korea, and the grandson of Kim Il-sung, the first Supreme Leader. He was officially declared the Supreme Leader at the death of his father in 2011. He was schooled in Switzerland, where he was described as shy and a basketball fan. It is said he had a fascination with the U.S. National Basketball Association and with Michael Jordan. He then went to Kim Il-sung University and obtained a degree in physics and another degree as an Army officer at the Kim Il-sung Military University. He is reported to smoke Yves Saint Laurent cigarettes, drink Johnnie Walker whisky, and drives a Mercedes-Benz 600 sedan. Kim has been very active in purging anyone from his government that he views as a threat. It is said he is trying to erase all traces of his father's rule. He ordered the execution of his uncle, Jang Sung-tack, by machine gun. In addition, Kim attempted to destroy all traces of Jang's existence by executing all of his family, including the children and grandchildren of all close relatives. It is said that Kim is obsessed with basketball and computer games. In 2013 Kim met ex-NBA superstar Dennis Rodman. Many think this was the first American he had ever met.

North Korea is an atheist state. Supreme Leader Kim Jong-un does not tolerate worship of anyone other than himself.

•••

The Following Day

Kim was meeting with the authors of 'The Anchor Crosses' report, Choe Yong-ho and Ri Yong-nam. Choe and Ri stood rigidly at attention in front of Kim's desk. General O Kuk-mu, supreme commander of the North Korean army, sat on a couch beside the desk.

Kim said, "I have read your report with great interest. If I understand correctly, anyone wearing one of these golden anchor crosses seems to be protected from any harm. Is that correct?"

"Yes Supreme Leader," Choe and Ri said in unison.

"Where does the power come from?" asked Kim.

Choe and Ri looked at each other, then Ri said, "The power is attributed to the gold having been blessed by the prophet, Jesus Christ."

Kim then reached inside the drawer of his desk, withdrew his pistol, and shot Ri in the forehead. Ri staggered a moment, then dropped to the floor dead.

Choe started to tremble. He closed his eyes.

"I will ask again," said Kim. "Where does the power come from?"

Choe opened his eyes, and mumbled, "It is unknown, Supreme Leader. The golden artifacts just seem to possess the power."

Kim said, "Has it been established that all of them possess the power?"

Choe replied, "Yes, Supreme Leader, there are documented stories that each has exhibited the power."

Kim then again pushed the intercom button on his desk and said, "Send the clean-up team in here immediately."

"Immediately, Supreme Leader, it shall be done," came the reply.

The door to Kim's office flew open and two guards rushed in. One grabbed the corpse under each of its armpits and pulled it out of the office. The other had a mop bucket and mopped the blood from the tile floor. Kim looked at his watch; if they took more than one minute, they would be executed on the spot and replaced by a new clean-up team. They finished their jobs in 50 seconds and were gone.

Kim then said, "General O."

General O stood at attention and said, "Yes, Supreme Leader."

"Listen carefully to what I wish done," Kim said. "You will carefully select three of your best men to join you and Choe on a most important and secret mission. Choe will go on the mission because of his knowledge of the golden anchor crosses. You will lead the mission. The other three you select should all speak English and be devoted to me beyond any doubt. They should be in perfect physical condition and of average size. You will divide them into two teams. You will lead one team, and your second in command will lead the other team. You will have exactly four weeks to prepare for your mission. Four weeks from today you will leave for the United States. Each team will travel independently. Two or three people traveling together will not be challenged. Five could raise suspicions. You will get fake identification, passports, and visas. Use our best government sources to prepare these. They must be flawless. You will get western suits and casual clothing. You will get western luggage. Each must be capable of passing as a salesman. Get business cards and any other required paperwork to support their stories. You will travel to the university in the town where the golden anchor crosses are located. You will devise a plan to steal them. You must steal them from where they are kept at the university and not try to steal them while they are being worn. No one has been successful doing that. The power they possess protects anyone wearing them, so it will be necessary to steal them when they are stored and not being worn. Do you understand?"

"I understand, Supreme Leader," replied General O. "May I ask what we are to do with these golden anchor crosses once we have them in our possession?"

"Ah, a wise question," Kim replied. "That will be my mission over the next three weeks. I will determine exactly what you will do when you get them, and I'll brief your teams before you leave for the U.S. I will see you and the other four members of your teams exactly three weeks from today at this same time. I will then tell you your mission with the golden anchor crosses."

"Yes, Supreme Leader, I am deeply honored to be chosen for such an important mission." said General O.

"That is all," Kim said.

General O and Choe turned and marched out of Kim's office.

•••

Kim was tired after the meeting, so he went to one of his chambers in the palace and took a nap for a couple of hours. Upon waking, he decided he needed a bit of exercise. His gout was not too painful at the moment, so he summoned a guard to push his wheelchair to his private gymnasium. He would shoot basketball for a little exercise. He then told the guard to summon the players. He had several members of the army that he had chosen to play basketball with him. Actually, the players mainly just retrieved the ball for him. Kim would stand at various places on the court and shoot the ball. Most of the time he missed, but occasionally he made a bucket. When he did the players would loudly cheer, "Supreme Leader is the best, Supreme Leader is the best!"

The players arrived on the court and greeted Kim. There was a new member with them today, and he was introduced to Kim. One of the regulars was ill, and the players knew that Kim always demanded each one of them stand in a particular position in order to retrieve the ball no matter where it bounced. Kim nodded to the new player.

He got up out of his wheelchair and started his ritual of shooting at various spots on the court. He had missed every shot he had taken, and was getting perplexed. He then was passed the ball to take a shot from a location immediately behind where the new player was standing. When Kim attempted to shoot the new player made a very bad mistake.... he raised his hands up to block the Supreme Leader's shot.

It was an instinctive move on his part, just intended to make Kim think he had opposition. The basketball hit the finger tips of the new player, and fell to the floor.

Kim reached down to his holster, pulled his pistol, and shot the new player squarely in the forehead. His head jerked around, and he fell to the floor dead.

Kim calmly said to the other players, "Get the clean-up team in here to haul this moron out."

"Yes, Supreme Leader," all of the other players said at once, and several started running to get the requested assistance.

In just a moment the clean-up team came running into the gym. The body and blood were removed in only 45 seconds this time.

Kim continued to shoot basketball with the players retrieving the ball for him. None of them tried blocking his shots.

●●●

One week later

Seoyeon Yi worked in a Pyongyang research laboratory. She was a very gifted student, and had graduated with high honors in biochemistry from Kim Il-Sung University. Seoyeon was now 35 years old, and had for the past several years yearned to be free from the oppression of the North Korean state. Her loyalties had gradually shifted away from the

Supreme Leader, and her goal was now to find some way to leave her country and eventually become a citizen of the United States. She knew that such thoughts could result in her execution if discovered by any government official, so she harbored all such thoughts to herself.

She had been assigned a project at her laboratory to develop a pill that would be effective as an antidote against an extremely toxic gas called TENX. Another laboratory in North Korea had worked for years to develop the TENX gas, and had perfected it about six months ago. It was so powerful that a vial of it only about 2 inches long and one half inch in diameter was capable of killing within 30 seconds any living being in a large room. When the TENX was released from the vial it spread into the atmosphere at a miraculous speed and was absorbed immediately into the skin of anyone it encountered. It found its way into the blood stream and caused immediate paralysis and heart failure. The North Korean army had plans to use TENX for both military and civilian purposes.

Seoyeon Yi had worked extremely hard for the past 6 months in developing an effective antidote against TENX. The pill she developed was amazingly effective. One minute after being swallowed it rendered the person taking it immune from the effects of TENX for a period of 30 minutes. The antidote was called ADX.

General O was familiar with the TENX program, and when Kim Jong-un assigned him to head up the program to get the six anchor crosses he immediately thought he might have use for the poison. He had requested that the Supreme

Leader allow him to conduct a test that would demonstrate its effectiveness. That demonstration was getting ready to occur.

Kim and General O were seated in a room looking through a thick glass window into another large room where two persons were seated, one a male and the other a female, who had been convicted of activity not in the best interest of the state. The couple had been caught by government officials emailing to friends in South Korea. They had been immediately put in prison. Today they served as subjects in the demonstration that was about to occur. As Kim and General O watched through the glass window, a door opened in the observed room and a soldier walked in carrying a vial of TENX in one hand and one ADX pill in the other hand. The door was closed behind him, and he walked to a desk where the two subjects were seated. He placed the tiny TENX vial on the table and then placed the ADX pill in his mouth and swallowed it. He then waited for one minute, after which he reached for the vial and broke the end of it to release the TENX gas into the room. Within just a few seconds the subjects both started to twitch, froth at the mouth, then violently start to jerk, and finally their eyes rolled up and they became limp and fell to the floor dead. The soldier watched without being affected. He then walked to the door, opened it, left the room and shut the door.

Kim looked at General O and said, "Very impressive! I assume you want to take a vial of TENX and ADX pills with you on your mission."

General O replied, "Yes, Supreme Leader, I think we could

possibly use it in capturing the anchor crosses. With your permission I will take them with me."

"A wise choice," Kim replied. "I will order it done."

•••

Two weeks later

Into Supreme Leader Kim Jong-un's office marched five persons. General O led the procession, followed by General Du Kyung-gu, Bin Yo-han, Seo Chi-won, and Choe Yong-ho. General O and General Du stood immediately before Kim's desk. The other three stood in a line behind them. All stood rigidly at attention.

Kim said, "All your plans are made as I ordered?"

General O replied, "Yes, Supreme Leader, exactly as you ordered."

"You have two teams, and I assume the one standing next to you will lead the second team?" asked Kim.

"Yes, Supreme Leader," replied General O, "he is General Du Kyung-gu."

"Very well," replied Kim. "As I ordered, exactly one week from today each team will leave for the U.S. Tell me your plans."

General O replied, "Myself, Bin Yo-han, and Choe Yong-ho will depart at 6 a.m. one week from today and will drive to Beijing, China. All our papers are in order, and there should be no problem crossing into China and then on to Beijing.

The drive should take about nine hours. We have tickets to fly from Beijing to Atlanta, Georgia, in the U.S. We will rent a car and drive to Lexington, Kentucky, which will take about six hours. We then have reservations at a hotel called the Hyatt, in downtown Lexington. We will then start to investigate how we will steal the golden anchor crosses from the university."

"Good," replied Kim. "And the second team?"

General Du spoke, "Supreme Leader, our team, consisting of Seo Chi-won and I will do exactly the same as General O's team except we will leave one day later. I thought that would minimize the possibility of detection."

Kim reached into his desk, pulled out his pistol, and shot General Du in the forehead. He staggered backward and fell to the floor dead. Kim then punched his intercom button and said, "Send in the clean-up team, immediately."

"Yes, Supreme Leader," came the response from the intercom.

The door to Kim's office opened and the clean-up team rushed in, one dragged General Du out of the office and the other mopped up the blood. This time it was accomplished in 40 seconds.

"My orders were that both teams would leave for the U.S. exactly one week from today, General Du did not follow that order. Replace him," Kim said.

"Yes, Supreme Leader, it will be done!" said General O. "We have a back-up team leader, General Sin Ji-hae. He is knowledgeable of all our planning and can step in to replace Du. General Sin's team will leave in another vehicle at the same time my team leaves. I'm sure we won't be identified as being together."

"Very well," Kim replied. He then reached again into his desk. General O's face turned pale.

Kim pulled a phone from his desk and said, "This is a very special, secure satellite phone. You will use it to report to me every day. I do not want to be inconvenienced, so you will call me exactly at midnight your time, which will be noon here in Pyongyang." Kim handed the phone to General O.

Blood started to return to General O's face, and he said, "It shall be done, Supreme Leader."

"I will give you my orders for how you will use the golden anchor crosses after you have them in your possession. Do you understand?" asked Kim.

"I understand, Supreme Leader. When I call you at midnight on the day that we steal the golden anchor crosses, you will tell me how to proceed."

"Correct," said Kim. "And one last thing, be sure that both teams take chains to attach to the golden anchor crosses. Just as soon as you get them in your possession, insert the chains through the hole in the anchor crosses and wear them around your necks. That way, each of you will be protected from any harm as you escape the university."

"It is understood, Supreme Leader," responded General O.

Kim then again punched the intercom button and said, "Bring me four quarter pounders with cheese, a large order of fries, and a large chocolate milk shake."

"It will be done, Supreme Leader," came the voice on the other end of the intercom.

When Kim was a young student attending school in Switzerland, he was exposed to western fast-food. There was a McDonald's restaurant located only two blocks from Kim's school. He became addicted to their menu. After becoming Supreme Leader, he ordered a team of chefs to travel to that same Swiss McDonald's and carefully sample and be able to reproduce everything on their menu. The team took four weeks to accomplish their mission. Each member of the team gained 12 pounds. They then returned to Pyongyang and developed a kitchen complete with all the McDonald foods ready to be prepared for the Supreme Leader at his beckoning call.

General O and the other four remained standing at rigid attention.

As he waited for his food, Kim reached again into his desk. The blood again drained from the faces of all five men. This time he extracted an iPod, and began playing a computer game, killing time until his food arrived. The blood returned to the faces of the five men.

After about ten minutes, the door to Kim's office opened, and a man in a chef's uniform stepped in carrying a tray with Kim's food order. The tray was placed on his desk. Kim then slowly ate all 4 quarter pounders with cheese, the large order of fries, and drank his chocolate milk shake. It took him a total of about 45 minutes to complete his meal. He continued to play the computer games as he ate. When finished, he belched, farted, and then looked at the five men still standing before him rigidly at attention and said, "Dismissed."

General O, Bin Yo-han, Seo Chi-won, and Choe Yong-ho

all did an about face and marched from Kim's office.

● ● ●

6 Days later

The Supreme Leader had just been served breakfast in his office. It consisted of a five egg, ham, bacon, and cheese omelet, cheese grits (which he had learned to love while in school in Switzerland), four pieces of buttered toast, three biscuits with gravy, jelly, marmalade, and coffee. As he ate his food the morning paper was delivered by one of his servants. The headline read:

Final Anchor Cross Discovered in Italy
Authenticated in U.S.

He spilled his coffee. He pushed the intercom button and said, "Get in here and take this food and get General O in here in the next 10 minutes.

"Immediately, Supreme Leader."

Eight minutes later General O entered into Kim's office.

"Have you seen the news?" asked Kim

"Not today, Supreme Leader," replied General O. "I normally do not read the newspaper until mid-morning."

Kim then said, "They found the sixth anchor cross, and it has been taken to Dr. Peters' center in Kentucky. He now has six of them. This calls for a change in plans. You will immediately add another person to General Sin Ji-hae's team. Now each team consists of three members. You leave on your mission as scheduled tomorrow.....so get the new member up and running and provided all necessary documentation. You will now recover six anchor crosses rather than five. All other orders remain the same."

"It shall be done, Supreme Leader," replied General O. "Ryu Jae-gyu is a back-up whom we can place immediately on General Sin Ji-hae's team. As a back-up he already has all the necessary training and documentation. Both teams will leave as you designated in the morning. I feel certain we will be successful Supreme Leader."

"You damn well better be," Kim replied. "On your way out tell my guards to bring me another breakfast....I feel my appetite returning."

"Yes Supreme Leader," replied General O as he turned to leave.

Chapter 4

Harlan County, Kentucky

The Slusher brothers were sitting in rocking chairs on the porch of their very large country home. The home was situated on a 50 acre plot of land about midway between Harlan and Cumberland, Kentucky. When approaching the home off highway 119 the private driveway wound around for about a mile before coming to a guard building with a gate across the road. Visitors were admitted by the guard, a fellow named Charlie, only with permission from one of the Slusher brothers. The entire 50 acres were secured by a seven foot high chain-link fence with barbed-wire strung along its top. The Slusher brothers did not welcome uninvited visitors.

Gunsmoke and Booger Slusher were fifty-two and fifty years-old, respectively. They were brought up as kids in a very poor coal mining town just north of Cumberland. They lived with their parents in a home owned by the coal company that George Slusher had worked for his entire life. George and Daisy were blessed with the two boys, although they had also hoped for a daughter, but that didn't happen. When the boys were in high school their father became very ill from black lung, and passed away the same year that the oldest boy, called Gunsmoke, graduated from Benham High School.   He and his younger brother, called Booger, both started to work in the mine where their father had worked. Daisy objected, but not too strongly, because she knew their options were very limited. George had passed away without any insurance and very little in savings. The family required money, so the boys began working in the coal mine. They had worked there for about 15 years when Daisy suddenly died from a stroke. One week after their mother's funeral, Gunsmoke purchased a lottery ticket from the grocery store near their home. He normally didn't buy lottery tickets, but for some strange reason had felt the urge to purchase one. It was an excellent urge! After deducting taxes, Gunsmoke was presented with a check for just over 100 million dollars. He had hit the super lottery and nation-wide he was the sole winner. At the time he won, winners were not required to reveal their identity, which was what Gunsmoke elected to do. He and his brother quietly quit their jobs and moved from the family home. Although previously very poor and not well educated, the brothers were very smart, and they greatly valued their privacy. And their luck continued when they selected at random a financial advisor out of the Knoxville, Tennessee phone book. Mr. August J. Richenberger, principal at Richenberger Financial, was a gentleman of highest integrity. After receiving the phone call from Gunsmoke, he immediately dropped everything he was doing and headed for Harlan County to meet with the Slushers. He had now served as their financial advisor for almost 20 years, and the arrangement had worked well.

Although it seemed a miracle, it was a fact that Gunsmoke Slusher had hit the super lottery and managed to keep it under wraps. Just as soon as he realized he had won he paid a visit to the grocery store where he had purchased the ticket and had a long talk with the owner. He told him that he would give him $50,000 to keep his mouth shut about the lottery. The owner was already to receive a nice payment just for selling the ticket, but to get an additional $50,000 made him agree to never reveal that he sold it.   And he had kept his word. Although the Slushers didn't have many close friends, the ones they did have were simply told that they had made some good investments, and that seemed to satisfy them. Others would occasionally inquire about the large home and grounds, but the Slusher brothers always just told them the same thing.....that they had just been lucky on some investments. Their financial advisor, August J. Richenberger, had initially advised the brothers to put only a modest amount of money in Harlan banks.....because bank employees talked.....and to invest the vast majority of their money in a wide portfolio of his recommendation. They followed his advice with great success. The brothers drove modest pick-up trucks, and made it a point not to make lavish purchases that could be traced to them. They did everything they could to keep a normal lifestyle. And they had been very successful at it for about 20 years.

In addition to Charlie, the brothers employed two other security employees. Charlie and George alternated shifts on the main gate. Charlie worked six a.m. to three p.m. George then worked from three until midnight. From midnight to six a.m. the gate was locked with no guard on duty. The third guard, Ray, patrolled the perimeter of the property during daylight hours and ran errands as requested by the brothers. The three guards were single and lived in a guest house located a short distance from the front gate. Gunsmoke and Booger had known all three since their days together at Benham High School. They were very good and devoted friends.

James Robert Slusher loved to watch the television series called 'Gunsmoke'. He watched it so much as a kid that his family and friends started calling him by the nickname Gunsmoke. He had answered to that name since his middle school days. Jay Alan Slusher entered into the world two years after James Robert. His mother Daisy took her first look at him and called him a real booger. Several family and friends were present at the time, and had called him by the nickname Booger since his birth. The brothers loved their nicknames, and very few people had any idea what their real names were. They were simply Gunsmoke and Booger Slusher.

As they slowly rocked back and forth in their rocking chairs, Gunsmoke said, "Brother, I do believe we have company. I think I see ole Gus Richenberger's car coming up the driveway."

Other than one of the guards, the only person allowed to pass through the front gate without permission of one of the brothers was August J. Richenberger. He had secured their total trust.

"Believe you're right, Gunsmoke," answered Booger. "You called him to come talk about those anchor cross things, if I recollect correctly."

"You do," said Gunsmoke. "Ole Gus always answers our calls promptly."

"He should, considering what we pay him," replied Booger.

"Worth his weight in gold to us," said Gunsmoke. "We should thank the good Lord every day for Gus Richenberger. Without him we likely would be either dead or broke, or both."

"Yeah, I know that," said Booger. "The good Lord was looking out for us when we made contact with Gus. He hasn't steered us wrong yet."

August J. Richenberger drove his new black Lexus up to the front of the house and parked. He got out of the car, carrying a briefcase, and shouted to the brothers, "Hey there my friends. As always, it's good to see you two. May I join you?"

Booger smiled and nodded affirmatively. Gunsmoke said, "By all means. We've been waiting for you. Have a seat."

Gus pulled another rocking chair up beside the brothers, and placed it so he would be facing them and sat. He then said, "August J. Richenberger at your service. What can I do for you?"

"Booger and I have been following those golden anchor cross things that the fellow Dr. Peters has in Lexington. The stories have been all over the news, both on television and in the newspapers. I'm sure you've seen them," Gunsmoke said.

"Yes I have," replied Gus. "They're hard to miss. I guess the latest reported that the last of them was found. I think it was the one that belonged to the Roman Emperor Constantine the Great. That was quite a find. If I recall correctly that makes a total of six of them that have been found by Dr. Peters at the University of Kentucky."

"That's my understanding," said Gunsmoke. "And I guess you know that they all seem to possess some kind of extraordinary power that protects anyone wearing one of them."

Gus said, "Yes, I have read those stories. They do indeed seem to be capable of protecting those that wear them, but only if their intentions are peaceable. Each one of them bears the Roman inscription **Pax Tecum**, which translates as 'Peace be with you'. Why are you interested, if I might ask?"

Gunsmoke replied, "Well, Booger and I have a bit of a hang-up on our privacy and security, as you are well aware. We're always concerned that our net worth might be discovered by someone and then that they would try and capture one or both of us in some kind of scheme to get our money. After hearing about those anchor cross things it occurred to us that if we each had one we could wear it and would always be safe. No harm could come to us."

Gus looked a bit shocked, and said, "Yes, I'm sure that is

true. But frankly I would doubt seriously that you could swing any kind of deal to obtain two of them. My understanding is that they are each priceless, and each one is still owned by someone who is allowing Dr. Peters to keep them temporarily in order to do further research related to them. What exactly did you have in mind?"

Gunsmoke said, "Gus, I'm sure in that briefcase there you have a statement that says where we currently stand with all our investments. Could you look at it and give us the number?"

"Sure thing, Gunsmoke," Gus replied. He opened the briefcase, looked through some papers, and then said, "Here it is. Your total current investments are worth $342,273,009."

Gunsmoke said, "We started some twenty years ago with about 100 million. We've managed to spend a goodly amount over the past twenty years, but we still have about three and one-half times as much as we did to start with! You've really done an excellent job of investing our money, Gus."

"Thank you," Gus said. "It's been a real pleasure working with you."

"Here's what we want to do," said Gunsmoke. "I want you to phone that guy Dr. Peters at U.K. I want you to tell him that you represent two brothers that wish to donate one million dollars to his Center. And be sure he understands that we wish to remain anonymous. Tell him we would like to meet with him to present the check. The three of us will then go to Lexington to meet with him. In our meeting, after we've presented him the check we will then raise the question of whether he thinks we might be able to purchase two of the anchor crosses, and that we would be willing to pay 25 million dollars for each one. Booger and I think that there might be two owners that would rather have 25 million dollars than ownership of an anchor cross. That's what we want to do."

Gus nodded and said, "I understand. I'll be happy to contact Dr. Peters and try and set up the appointment. I don't think there will be a problem with that. And then we'll just have to see what he says about your buying two of the anchor crosses. I really don't have any idea if it would be possible....but we can sure try."

Gunsmoke and Booger nodded in agreement. Just then a large, yellow tabby cat jumped from the porch into Booger's lap. Booger gently stroked the cat as it settled down, closed its eyes, swished its tail, and started to purr.

The Slusher brothers had always been cat lovers. They had cats in their home as they grew up, and had always been very fond of them. When they moved to their current home on the 50 acre plot, they brought three cats with them. They frequently visited the animal shelter, and on most such trips always came back home with at least one new cat. At last count they thought they had somewhere around 20. They loved their cats and gave them the very best of care. One of the saddest things occurred to them about 15 years ago when they lost one of their very favorite cats. Smoky was a large, gray tabby cat that they had brought home from the shelter about a year earlier when she was only a few months old. She was extremely smart, and very loving. One day she was out playing near the front gate when Ray came home from running an errand and Charlie opened the front gate for him. Smoky saw the gate open and ran through it before it closed. She wanted to explore outside the fenced area. It was a new experience for her. Charlie saw her flash through the gate, and he ran after her, but couldn't match her speed. That was the last anyone at the Slusher estate ever saw of Smoky. The brothers, along with Ray and George searched for several days looking for her, but with no luck. The brothers really loved ole Smoky, and they grieved for her for months. It was a very sad time; Smoky was gone.

The brothers continued to talk with Gus. Booger gently lifted the yellow tabby cat off his lap and placed it on the floor. He then walked inside to get everyone a glass of sweet tea. He returned with the tea and the three continued to chat.

Two large eyes appeared around the corner of the porch. They were attached to a bundle of gray fur. The very young kitten waddled over to Gunsmoke and began to rub against his leg. Gunsmoke reached down and lifted the kitten to his lap. He then petted the cat, and it started its motor. The purr was loud enough for all three men to hear. They all got satisfied looks on their faces.

As he petted the kitten, Gunsmoke said, "Little Fluffy here is our most recent acquisition. Ray found her wondering aimlessly around highway 119 just where you turn to come here. He stopped and called for her and she came running to him. I think she's made the adjustment to living here very nicely. The only bad thing about her is that she reminds Booger and me of ole Smoky. She has about the same coloring. That was sure a very sad time for us when Smoky disappeared. I think about it a lot. And to make things even worse, it was about the same time that a church about a mile from here burned. I've often wondered if maybe Smoky wondered to the church and somehow got caught-up in the fire. I guess we'll never know. Booger and I made an anonymous contribution to the church to enable them to rebuild. But what happened to Smoky remains a mystery."

Gunsmoke and Booger were strong Christians. They had been taken every Sunday by their parents to the Loving Arms Baptist Church in Benham starting when they were still in diapers. They each accepted the Lord Jesus Christ when they were in grade school, and they had been faithful followers ever since. After hitting the lottery and moving, they still continued to be active in the Benham church, attending every Sunday and serving on several committees. Starting the first year they had the lottery money they made an annual anonymous contribution to the Loving Arms Baptist Church of $250,000. It was set up by Gus Richenberger such that the check received by the church was a cashier's check that could not be traced. The brothers also had spent a great deal of time researching various charitable organizations, and with Gus's assistance made substantial contributions to select charities. They took great pride in being able to help people.

Gus turned his glass of sweet tea up to take the last sip. He placed the glass down and said, "Well boys, I think I've got my work cut out. I'll head back home and in the morning get started putting together all the paperwork we'll need for our trip to Lexington to visit with Dr. Peters. I'll keep you posted on my progress. Just as soon as I'm able to get us an appointment with him I'll give you a call so you can get it on your calendars. Anything else we need to talk about?"

"Don't think so, Gus," said Booger. "I think we've pretty much covered everything."

"You drive real careful back to Knoxville," Gunsmoke said to Gus. "There's a lot of nuts out there on the highway."

"Don't I know it," replied Gus. "You boys take care.....I'll be in contact."

Gus walked to his car, got in, and started the trip back to Knoxville. Gunsmoke and Booger continued to rock on their porch.

Chapter 5

Lexington, Kentucky

I t was a beautiful September morning. Daylight was just making its appearance across the magnificent Keeneland Thoroughbred Race Course. The morning warm-ups were underway. Maybe 25 horses were on the immaculate track being put through their paces by trainers, jockeys, and owners. The thoroughbreds were truly beauty in motion. They were without doubt one of the Lord's most stunning creations.

The Keeneland Race Course was located just outside the city of Lexington, across highway 60 from Lexington's Bluegrass Field Airport. Over the years, thousands upon thousands of visitors flying into Lexington had been treated to the unique beauty of Keeneland and its adjacent neighbor, the famed Calumet Farm, as they looked down from their plane making its final approach to land. A rare site indeed.

Keeneland was founded in 1936 on about 150 acres of choice Bluegrass farm land. It is truly the most beautiful race course in the U.S., if not the entire world. It has been ranked #1 of the top ten tracks in North America. Its beauty is stunning. The driving force behind the establishment of Keeneland was Mr. Jack Keene. The track has two annual racing events, one in April and one in October. Each lasts about three weeks. In addition to the race track, Keeneland has the world's largest Thoroughbred auction house. The Sales Pavilion is located in the center of the Keeneland property, just outside the race track. There are three annual sales conducted; the September Yearling Sale, the November Breeding Stock Sale, and the January Horses of All Ages Sale. Keeneland Sales boast of having sold 82 horses that won 88 Breeders' Cup World Championship races, 19 Kentucky Derby winners, 21 Preakness winners, 18 Belmont winners, and 11 recipients of the Eclipse Award as Horse of the Year.

There were perhaps a couple dozen spectators that had gotten up early enough to come watch the warm-ups this morning. Those were standing along the rail, most with cameras in hand, admiring and photographing the magnificent thoroughbreds as they passed by. Two persons were standing in a spot next to the rail without any cameras and had positioned themselves away from any of the others. They were dressed in jeans and knit shirts, and were wearing baseball-style caps; one with a Keeneland logo on it, the other with a UK logo. The two were talking to each other, and looked to the casual observers to be just two race fans enjoying the warm-ups. They were not.

The fellow wearing the hat with the Keeneland logo was Sheikh Mansour bin Ahmed Al Maktoum, Crown Prince of Dubai from the United Arabs Emirates (UAE). The other fellow, the one with the UK hat, was Adnan bin Saeed Al Amin, the Crown Prince's long-time, trusted friend who, among other duties, was in charge of the Royal Family's stables and equine operations in Dubai. The two were at Keeneland for the September Yearling Sale. They had arrived at Bluegrass Field yesterday morning in the Prince's private Boeing 737 jet, which was currently parked at the end of a runway only about 50 feet from highway 60, across which was the main entrance to Keeneland. After arriving, the two exited their jet and walked across the highway where they were greeted by Keeneland personnel driving an electric cart to take Mansour and Adnan to the Sales Pavilion. The Crown Prince then purchased 3 yearlings, for a total of 2.4 million dollars. A purchase he considered a real bargain. The two spent last night in a suite at a Lexington Hotel, and had returned this morning for an early departure back to Dubai. But only the Crown Prince would be flying back. Adnan would be staying a bit longer. But Before Mansour's departure they wanted to enjoy the beauty that was Keeneland a bit more, and to also go over Adnan's instructions one final time.

The Crown Prince said, "Adnan, my friend, I wish money could buy the beauty of Kentucky. If it could, I would purchase it and take it back to Dubai."

"I understand your feeling," said Adnan. "It is lovely beyond description. But I guess we will have to be content with taking the three magnificent yearlings back. I'm sure they will reward us greatly."

"As do I," said Mansour. "So before I depart, I would like to make sure you understand exactly my wishes regarding the acquiring of one of the golden anchor crosses."

• • •

The previous evening Mansour and Adnan had enjoyed a delicious meal at an exclusive Lexington restaurant. After their meal Mansour said, "I have a mission for you, Adnan, that will require you to remain here in Lexington for perhaps a few more days. Will that be okay with you?"

"Your wish is my command, Mansour. I shall be most happy to try and accomplish whatever it is you desire," replied Adnan.

"You are very faithful, Adnan," responded Mansour. "As I know you recall, there have been many attempts to kidnap me, and many other schemes attempting to abduct me in order to get portions of the royal family money. Fortunately, all have failed. But I continue to be very concerned that one of these days one might be successful. I know that you have heard all the news coverage related to the recovery of the golden anchor crosses that were produced by the Roman Emperor Constantine the Great. And I'm sure you are aware that there are now six of these, and that they currently reside right here in Lexington at a center, called the Center for Appalachian Research, that is a part of the University of Kentucky. The Director of that center is a Dr. Randy Peters. Dr. Peters has the six anchor crosses in order to study and conduct research related to them, but they are each individually owned. Their owners simply have agreed to allow Dr. Peters to retain possession so long as he has need of them for his research. The news stories that I have read about each of them document that the artifacts possess some kind of supernatural power capable of protecting those that wear them. If I had one of these golden anchor crosses I would not have to fear anyone trying to do me harm. It would be a great relief, and would permit me to do lots of things that I currently feel restrained from doing.   Do you understand?"

"Indeed. Yes, I certainly do," replied Adnan. "I think I can see a visit to Dr. Peters in my near future," Adnan said with a slight smile on his face.

"Your perception is correct," Mansour said.   "I have already taken the liberty of getting assistance from our good friend Tim Bassett, Keeneland's President, to call Dr. Peters to get you an appointment. Keeneland and the University of Kentucky are very supportive of each other. Keeneland, being a non-profit organization, contributes vast sums of money to charities and educational institutions, with the University of Kentucky being high on its list. Tim's phone call to Dr. Peter's office was very favorably received, and you have an appointment with him tomorrow at 2 p.m."

Mansour handed Adnan a card that had the appointment information on it, including the address of the Center for Appalachian Research.

"I will look forward greatly to meeting with Dr. Peters tomorrow afternoon. What, specifically, should I ask of him?" asked Adnan.

Monsour replied, "You can explain to him the reason why I would like to own one of the anchor crosses, as I have just discussed with you, and then tell him that we would be prepared to pay the asking price for the artifact, and will also donate an additional 10% as a gift to Dr. Peters' center. Surely at least one of the owners would be willing to sell their anchor cross, and they can set their price."

"A most generous offer, Monsour," said Adnan. "I will be happy to convey that information to him, and will give you a call just as soon as we end our meeting."

"I will be looking forward to hearing from you tomorrow, Adnan," answered Monsour.

•••

The Crown Prince then carefully went over again what he and Adnan had discussed the night before about securing a golden anchor cross from Dr. Peters.

"So, Adnan, do you have questions regarding your mission?" asked Monsour.

"I think I understand. I'll do all in my power to make it successful, and will give you a call promptly when I conclude meeting with Dr. Peters."

"Thank you, Adnan," said Monsour. "My jet will be back here to pick you up when you're ready."

The two men embraced. Monsour turned and walked to the electric cart that was to take him to his plane. Adnan walked to get a taxi to his hotel. The plan was set.

Chapter 6

Harlan, Kentucky

The mayor's office was small. It was located in city hall, but Mayor Fred Knapp seldom really used it. He owned Creech Cafe, located directly across the street from the Harlan County Court House, and most of his business as mayor was conducted there. Either in his small office in the back of the restaurant, or at a table in the cafe. Fred, now 73 years old, had been the popular Mayor of Harlan now for about 9 years. He had graduated from Harlan High School 54 years ago and immediately started working at Creech Cafe for his father. When his father passed away, Fred inherited the business and had continued to operate it very successfully. It was perhaps the most popular gathering spot in Harlan. School kids flooded into it after school each day, and old timers made drinking coffee and swapping tales there a daily ritual. Fred loved his jobs, both as owner of Creech

Cafe and as mayor of Harlan. There were two features of Creech Cafe that were unique. First, it had a resident parrot. Polly was a large, green bird that was now 25 years old. She normally resided on a perch that Fred had built for her near the entrance door. Polly had quite a vocabulary, and would frequently greet customers as they entered the door. She also had quite an appetite, and would mooch food from any client willing to share. Everyone in Harlan loved Polly. Many years ago there was a health inspector that took a dim view of having a parrot in a food establishment and had given Fred a citation. He appealed it, and at the Health Department hearing most of the people in Harlan showed up to support Polly. He won the appeal and the issue had never again presented itself. Polly was a part of Creech Cafe. The second unique feature of the restaurant was its wall coverings. From its outset Fred's father, and later Fred, had posted interesting articles and photos on the walls. Once posted, these were seldom ever removed. All the walls in the cafe were plastered with newspaper articles, features from magazines, and photographs from every possible source. There were so many of these that it was almost impossible to determine the color of the wall behind them. Fred was familiar with every one, and loved to tell his curious customers the stories behind them. He could spend hours relating these. It was his favorite hobby.

Among Creech's many regular patrons were the Harlan County sheriff, J. Bert Sterling, and his deputies. The sheriff's office was located directly across Central Street in the Harlan County Courthouse. The 63 year old sheriff joined the sheriff's department upon graduating from Harlan High School. He served about 15 years as a deputy, and then decided to place his name on the ballot for sheriff. He won overwhelmingly, and had continued to do so in all subsequent elections. He was extremely popular. Everyone thought him to be honest, hard working, and fair. He was what a sheriff should be. He was totally devoted to his job, and for that reason had never married, although many single ladies in Harlan had indicated an interest. Bert was handsome. He was tall and slim, and always dressed immaculately in his uniform. He was, most of the time, warm and friendly, but when apprehending crooks could be hard as nails. For several years now he had dated Carolyn Potter, a teller at the Miners Bank in Harlan. Carolyn's son Kyle was Bert's chief deputy.

It was Deputy Kyle Potter who, when he was 10 years old, was exploring in a remote mountainous area of Harlan County and stumbled upon the 1798 ruins of Reverend Karl Seibert's covered wagon. Kylie, as he was known then, found in these ruins the first of what would be six golden anchor crosses. He was wearing the anchor cross when, while visiting his mother at the Miners Bank, it first demonstrated its amazing and mysterious power by saving the lives of himself, his mother, and several bank employees when several crooks, one of whom was Kyle's father, attempted to rob the bank. Strangely the would-be robbers were rendered unconscious when they tried to seal Kylie and the bank employees in a vault. This, if successful, would have suffocated them. During this botched robbery Sheriff Sterling discovered 3.5 million dollars the robbers had gathered from lock boxes belonging to Pretty Boy Maggard, Harlan's most notorious drug dealer. This money was then designated by the courts as follows: [1] one million dollars to Harlan County for the construction of the Seibert Anchor Cross Memorial building on the Northwest corner of the court house property, [2] one million dollars to the U.K. Center for Appalachian Research earmarked for anchor cross study, and [3] 1.5 million dollars to Kylie Potter in a trust fund controlled by his mother, Carolyn, until his 21st birthday. After graduating from Harlan High School, Kyle entered the Criminal Justice Program at Eastern Kentucky State University in Richmond, Kentucky, from which he graduated with honors. Sheriff Sterling had a vacancy in his office when his chief deputy, Ape Cornett, resigned in order to pursue a career with the Kentucky State Police. Bert filled this vacancy with Kyle Potter, where he had served most effectively now for about three years. Bert and Kyle were super friends as well as excellent lawmen.

Sheriff Sterling's office was small due to a very limited budget. The population of Harlan County had been in a constant decline since 1940, due largely to shrinking jobs attributable to the decreased demand for coal along with increased automation to mine it. The 1940 census showed the county with 75,275 persons, but by 2010 it was down to 29,278. Other than coal, government checks were about the only other significant source of money in Harlan County. The impact was certainly felt by the sheriff's budget, as the tax base dwindled. The office had only six employees in Harlan, and another five at a satellite office located in Cumberland, about 25 miles Northeast of Harlan on highway 119. The

Harlan office only had two shifts, one from 8 a.m. to 4:30 p.m. and another from 4:30 p.m. to midnight. From midnight to 8 a.m. any calls that came into the sheriff's office were directed to the Kentucky State Police. In addition to Sheriff Sterling the Harlan office had deputies Kyle Potter, Rosie Cain, Simpson Brown, Mousy Giles, and Bill Black. The sheriff, Kyle, Rosie, and Simpson usually worked the first shift; Mousy and Bill the second.

There was one other significant presence in the Harlan County Sheriff's Department. She was a 15 pound gray tabby cat named Preacher Puss. Deputy Rosie Cain normally worked the first shift and usually took care of all the paperwork, served as dispatcher, and assisted anyone coming to the office. She also took care of Preacher Puss. She loved Preacher Puss. It had all begun about 15 years ago when the cat was rescued by firemen when she was discovered in the back room of a church that had caught fire. She was screaming at the top of her lungs. After finding her the firemen took her to a vet to be checked out. After examination the vet said she was fine..... she had just inhaled a lot of smoke. The firemen then asked around the church seeking the cat's owner, but without luck. They then took her to the Sheriff's office. It was love at first sight! Just as soon as Rosie laid eyes on the beautiful gray cat there was a strong mutual bond. After the firemen told Rosie the story about the cat, she immediately proclaimed her name as Preacher Puss. She did this because the cat was found screaming in a church. Rosie begged Sheriff Sterling to keep the cat, and Bert somewhat reluctantly agreed. She then rushed to Wal-Mart and purchased all the necessary bedding, food, and supplies for Preacher Puss, including a good supply of the cat treats called 'Whisker Lickins'. The then chief deputy Ape Cornett built the cat a shelf above his desk and beside the entrance door. Preacher Puss immediately accepted her new digs, and just loved to lay on the shelf, purr, swish her tail, and watch all the goings-on in the sheriff's office. Those that came to know her always gave her a good pet as they walked into the department, and she always rewarded them with a loud meow and a big tail swish. Soon after she was adopted it was learned that she had a strange peculiarity: she hated guns! This was first discovered a few days after the cat's arrival when Deputy Cornett started to clean his pistol. When he pulled the gun from its holster Preacher Puss immediately started screaming and jumped from her shelf onto the top of the deputy's head. Her claws were out, and they dug into his head. All her long gray hair fell down over his face. The deputy didn't have a clue what had happened, but he did know he was in pain with some kind of injury to his head and blood was streaming down his face. When he dropped the gun Preacher Puss immediately withdrew her claws and jumped back up to her shelf, laid down, closed her eyes, and started to purr. Rosie ran over from behind her counter. She was startled by the cat's behavior, but couldn't help but get a little smile on her face when she saw the cat jump back to her shelf and settle down. After trying to calm Ape down she retrieved the first aid kit and took care of his scratches. The deputies really didn't understand exactly what had happened, but just a few days later a person entered the department with the intention of robbing them with a drawn gun. Preacher Puss repeated her performance, and it was then that Rosie figured out that the cat had some kind of hang-up about guns. Her reaction when she saw a gun was to scream and jump with claws extended on the head of the person holding it. It was very effective, and had been repeated numerous times over the years. Sheriff Sterling quickly saw the usefulness of the cat, and he proclaimed Preacher Puss to be among his best deputies and on one occasion threatened to put her in uniform. He also loved the fact that she only cost him for food and Whisker Lickins. Preacher Puss's reputation grew among not only the law enforcement community but also among all the people of Harlan. Preacher Puss was one-of-a-kind! She had found her place!

Today Mayor Knapp was sitting in his office at city hall. Sheriff Sterling was with him. The sheriff had known Fred since his middle school days when he, along with lots of other school friends, would visit Creech Cafe after school. The two had become very close friends over the years. Fred said, "Bert, I thank you for coming over. I wanted to talk with you here where we wouldn't be disturbed. Something's come up that we need to deal with, and I need your advice."

"Always glad to help, Mr. Mayor," replied Bert. "What's going on?"

"It's all this stuff with that new anchor cross. I know you've seen it on television and read the newspaper reports. Randy Peters called me yesterday morning before his news conference to give me a 'heads-up'. Now that the sixth and final anchor cross has been discovered, it changes everything for our upcoming Anchor Cross Festival next month. Just when I thought we had the agenda all set for it, this huge development occurs. And right now I just don't know how we should handle it."

The first annual Anchor Cross Festival, or ACFes, was held on October 6th of last year. It was established at the recommendation of Kentucky's Governor Brad Shear in hopes that it would be very successful in drawing large numbers of people to Harlan. Lots of people meant lots of money spent, and economic development was a prime consideration. It had been extremely successful. A record number of people crowded into Harlan for all the activities, the highlight of which was to have on display all the anchor crosses in the Seibert Memorial on the Harlan Court House grounds. Planning started immediately after the first ACFes for ACFesII, which was now only about 3 weeks away.

"I'm not sure I'm following you, Fred," Bert replied.

Fred answered, "Well, look at this way. Our festival is all about the anchor crosses. We already had everything set to once again have Randy bring the five he had in his possession to Harlan to be on display for the festival, and we had all the various programs set that were to take place on the stage to be erected on the court house steps. Now the whole world has been made aware that the final anchor cross has been found and is in the possession of Dr. Randy Peters. Anyone considering coming to ACFesII would certainly expect to see the new one.....the Constantine anchor cross. And the thing is, it's owned by the Italian government. I don't know if we could possibly get approval for its inclusion in our festival in the short time we have. But without it, our festival could go down the tubes."

"Oh, mayor, I think you're over reacting," Bert replied. "We've still got three weeks. That should be plenty of time to make the arrangements. I know Randy would do all in his power to make it happen. I think you just need to proceed with all the plans for it to be included, and to get rolling with whatever requests are required to Italy. I think it'll be fine."

Dr. Randy Peters had a special place in his heart for Harlan. After receiving his Doctorate Degree in anthropology from the University of Virginia he accepted an appointment at the University of Kentucky on their anthropology faculty. After five years he was appointed the Director of U.K.'s new Center for Appalachian Research, a position he had held now for about twenty-three years. Randy had grown particularly fond of Harlan as he was doing his doctoral dissertation addressing the history of Harlan County. And then when the Seibert anchor cross was found there and Kyle and Carolyn Potter asked their pastor, Raymond Bell, his advice, Pastor Bell immediately recommended that they contact Dr. Peters because of his expertise on Harlan's history. From that contact and his subsequent research Randy had developed into the leading expert on the anchor crosses, and his center was the focal point for related study and research.

Raymond Bell was pastor of New Hope Baptist Church in Harlan. He and Randy Peters had met at a seminar Randy was presenting in Lexington addressing the history of Appalachia. At that time Raymond and his wife Betty were working in Lexington, and Raymond had just completed his Master of

Theology degree at nearby Asbury Theological Seminary in Wilmore, Kentucky. Randy and the Bells became close friends. Randy heard about the vacancy in the pulpit at New Hope Baptist in Harlan and mentioned to Raymond that he might wish to contact them. He did, and had now been their pastor for about sixteen years. He and Betty loved Harlan, and Harlan loved them.

Although last year was the first official Anchor Cross Festival, similar celebrations had begun two years before. The Seibert Anchor Cross Memorial building was built on the Harlan Court House property soon after Kyle Potter had discovered the first of the Savior's crosses. Twelve years later the second was found, the Pelle anchor cross, and its discovery sparked a celebration instigated by Mayor Knapp wherein the Seibert and the Pelle anchor crosses were displayed in the Memorial building after being unveiled in a ceremony on a stage constructed on the steps of the Harlan County Court House. Lots of people attended, so when the Helena anchor cross was discovered several months later, the mayor elected to have another celebration that would include the three artifacts. It too was a huge success. It was then that Kentucky's governor, Brad Shear, elected to sponsor and promote an Anchor Cross Festival in Harlan on the first weekend of October each year. It would be held this year with limited activities starting on Friday, October 4th, the major activities on Saturday, October 5th, and concluding events on Sunday, October 6th.

Chapter 7

Lexington, Kentucky

Joyce walked into Randy's office with her appointments calendar in hand. It was 8:30 a.m. She said, "Dr. Peters, you have a busy day today. In addition to several appointments with faculty, you have a 10 o'clock with two brothers named Slusher from Harlan County and their financial advisor, a Mr. August J. Richenberger. You then have a 2 o'clock with a Mr. Adnan bin Saeed Al Amin that was requested by Tim Bassett from Keeneland. Anything special I need to do in preparation for these?"

"I don't think so," replied Randy. "The 2 o'clock is a fellow from the United Arabs Emirates, and I really don't know what the appointment is all about. The 10 o'clock is the one that you set up when the Richenberger fellow called to say his clients wanted to make a one million dollar donation to the CAR. That sounded real good to me."

Joyce then said, "Well, let's keep our fingers crossed that they are both legit. I feel certain the 2 o'clock is, since Tim Bassett requested it. Probably has something to do with Keeneland, but I can't imagine what it would be. But I'm sure not certain about the 10 o'clock. Not too many folks show up with a one million dollar check in hand."

"We'll know in about an hour and a half," Randy said. "In the meantime, would you please phone Dr. Perilli in Naples. It's early afternoon over there, and I think he'll be expecting my call."

Joyce turned to leave the office and said, "Sure thing boss. I'll buzz you as soon as I get him."

Randy pulled a large file from his desk. The tab on the file read 'ACFesII'. A couple of days ago he had gotten a call from Mayor Knapp. Fred had sounded panicky, and Randy determined his concern was over the recent discovery of the Constantine anchor cross. He was worried that ACFesII, coming up now in a little less than three weeks, would not be a success unless the final anchor cross was included. Randy had told him to calm down, that he felt certain he could obtain permission from the Italian government to take the artifact to Harlan for the festival. He told the mayor he would first contact Governor Shear to get him to officially make the request via an overnight letter. Dr. Perilli had received the letter yesterday and had immediately emailed Randy to say that he thought it would certainly be granted, but that he had to make the official request to his superiors. He had then asked Randy to call him this morning (afternoon in Naples) to hopefully finalize the arrangement. Randy was anxious to get his response. If it was positive Randy planned to contact then the owners of all the other five anchor crosses to see if they could possibly attend ACFesII. If that happened, then this year's festival should go huge. It would celebrate and have on display all six of the Savior's crosses. And it might even be possible to have all the owners with them. Randy grinned as he thought of the enormous crowd that should attract to Harlan. Mayor Knapp would be the happiest man in the state. And to think he was concerned about the discovery of the new anchor cross! You just sometimes have to make lemonade out of lemons, Randy thought.

Randy's intercom startled him out of his thought. "Yes Joyce," he said

"I have Dr. Perilli on line one," Joyce replied.

"I'll get it. Thanks Joyce," said Randy.

"Dr. Perilli.....thank you for accepting my call," Randy said

"Please, call me Alfonso," replied Dr. Perilli. "It is my pleasure, especially so since I have very good news for you concerning the Constantine anchor cross!"

Randy got a huge smile on his face and said, "Oh, that must mean that permission has been granted to take it to the festival in Harlan.....I hope!"

"It has indeed," said Dr. Perilli. "The request to my superiors went all the way up to the President of our Republic. Because I stressed that time was of the essence, the request was expedited, and the President approved it. Not only that, but approval was given for both Dr. Eden and me to come to Kentucky to visit with you and to accompany you and the artifact to Harlan for the festival. I just gave Verla the news this morning and we are both now extremely excited and looking forward tremendously to meeting you and visiting in Kentucky."

"How wonderful," said Randy. "On my notepad before me I had noted to be sure to invite you to the festival if approval was granted for your anchor cross's participation. So, that question has been answered, and I must say I'm so very pleased that both the Constantine anchor cross and the two of you will be a part of ACFesII. And I'll certainly look forward to being able to show you as much of Kentucky as your schedule will allow."

"You are so kind," said Dr. Perilli. "Verla and I will start immediately making our trip arrangements, and I'll share those with you just as soon as we have them."

"Please do," responded Randy. "In the meantime I'm going to be contacting the owners of all the other anchor crosses to see if they could also participate with us.....it should be a really great time together."

"It certainly sounds that way," Dr. Perilli said. "Do take care, and Pax Tecum!"

Randy replied, "Pax Tecum to you, my friend." He gently hung up the telephone.

Randy then pulled out his cell phone and called Fred Knapp in Harlan. He relayed his conversation with Dr. Alfonso Perilli. Fred was so pleased he could hardly contain himself. And when Randy told him that he would be contacting the other anchor cross owners to try and have them all at the festival.....well, it was just about more than Mayor Knapp could take. Fred thanked Randy profusely. The two agreed to be in contact regarding all the festival arrangements.

Just as Randy told Fred good-bye, Joyce once again came on the intercom saying, "Dr. Peters, August J. Richenberger and the Slusher brothers are here for their appointment."

"Please send them in," he replied.

The door to Randy's office opened and in walked a gentleman dressed in what looked to be a very expensive suit and tie. Following behind him were two other gents, dressed in sport shirts and slacks.

August J. Richenberger walked to the side of Randy's desk, where he had stood to greet them, and stuck out his hand to Randy. The two exchanged a vigorous handshake as Richenberger said, "Dr. Peters, thank you so much for agreeing to talk with us. My name is August J. Richenberger," and he handed Randy his business card. "Please call me Gus. These two other gentlemen are the Slusher brothers, Gunsmoke and Booger. They live in Harlan County. I'm from Knoxville."

"Please, please.....have a seat gentlemen," Randy said after shaking hands with the brothers. "I look forward to talking with you."

"And we with you," Gus said. "I think you are aware that my clients desire to make a donation to your center, for the purpose of furthering your excellent research and study on the anchor crosses."

"I did have that understanding," replied Randy. "And the number I heard certainly caught my attention!"

"One million dollars," said Gunsmoke as Gus handed him the check. He then passed it to Randy.

Randy took the check and studied it. It appeared to be a cashier's check in the amount of one million dollars made payable to the University of Kentucky's Center for Appalachian Research. Randy studied the check for a moment, and then said, "This is very extraordinary. Certainly it isn't every day a check for a million dollars walks into my office. What do you want in exchange, if I might ask?"

Gus replied, "Absolutely nothing. The donation is given without strings. The only thing the brothers ask is for you to consider a request from them. You may agree or disagree to the request, but the check remains yours."

"Certainly an offer I couldn't refuse," Randy replied. "I'm anxious to hear the request."

Booger looked at Gunsmoke, then Gunsmoke said, "What Gus says about our donation is absolutely accurate. My brother and I have been very fortunate in our investments with Gus, and the donation is in appreciation for all the fine work you've done investigating those beautiful, golden anchor crosses. Since Booger and I are from Harlan County, we've certainly followed all the developments ever since the Seibert anchor cross was discovered by Kyle Potter. We've watched all the news on television and in the newspapers about all of them, including the recent one you discovered in Italy. The stories about them are truly remarkable."

"Thank you, Gunsmoke," said Randy. "And let me say I love your name.....I too was a big fan of Matt Dillon, Chester, Kitty, and Doc! You do certainly seem familiar with all the artifacts. What exactly is your request?"

Gunsmoke replied, "As I said, Dr. Peters, Booger and I have

been extremely fortunate in our investments, and I guess I must confess to you that we are both very concerned about our well-being and safety. It is our understanding that all six of the anchor crosses possess some kind of mysterious power that appears to protect from harm anyone wearing one. We also understand that all of them have separate owners. Our request is for you to inquire of the owners if they would be willing to sell their anchor cross. We would like to purchase two of them. We are prepared to pay 25 million dollars for each one. Our sole purpose for wanting to own these is to assure our safety. We would have no other use for them. All we ask is that you present our offer to the owners. Perhaps there might be two that would rather have 25 million dollars each than to own an anchor cross. Do you understand our request?"

"I think so," said Randy. "And I can't give you an answer, or even a guess, about whether two of the owners would consider selling. I can tell you that I would certainly be willing to present the question to them. We're currently hoping that all the owners will participate with us in the second annual anchor cross festival in Harlan on the weekend of October 5th. I think it would likely be best if I presented the question to all of them at one time, and I should be able to do that sometime during the festival period. Would that be too long for you to wait for an answer?"

Gunsmoke looked at Booger. Booger nodded affirmatively. Gunsmoke then said, "That would be just fine, Dr. Peters. And since we live close to Harlan, we'd be happy to attend the meeting should you wish."

"That might be a good idea," replied Randy. "Let me work on it and I'll get back to you with all the particulars. Should I contact you, or Mr. Richenberger?"

"Gus is a little easier to get in touch with than us," said Booger. "Just give him a call. Or if any other questions come up, he should be able to answer them as well."

"One last thing," said Gunsmoke. "We don't want any publicity from all this. Please agree not to release our names. The million dollar donation is anonymous. Is that agreeable?"

"Not a problem," replied Randy, and with a smile added, "Your identity will remain unknown to anyone other than the IRS."

"That's okay," Gus said with a big smile.

All stood and shook hands, and the visitors departed.

Randy sat at his desk and looked at the one million dollar check. He thought, 'This day has certainly gotten off to an excellent start!'

•••

Randy had an appointment with a member of the faculty at 11:30 a.m., and then the two of them went to lunch at the faculty club. After lunch he returned to his office and had a meeting with one of the university administrators from 1:15 to 1:45 p.m. He now sat at his desk awaiting the arrival of his 2 o'clock appointment with the fellow from the UAE.

At exactly 2 p.m. Joyce announced on the intercom the

arrival of Adnan bin Saeed Al Amin. He was ushered into Randy's office.

Randy stood and shook hands with Mr. Al Amin. He then said, "Please, have a seat. I was pleased to get the call from Tim Bassett to arrange for this appointment, although I must admit he didn't really say the purpose of your visit."

Al Amin responded, "Thank you Dr. Peters. Please call me Adnan. I thank you for allowing me to meet with you, and I'm certainly indebted to Mr. Bassett for arranging our meeting. He didn't tell you the purpose of the meeting because he did not know. He was simply doing a favor for my boss, the crown prince of Dubai, Sheikh Mansour bin Ahmed Al Maktoum. As I imagine you are well aware, the Prince does a lot of business with Keeneland."

"Oh yes, I'm certainly aware of that. He's a frequent visitor at the horse sales, and often goes back to the UAE with several prize race horses," replied Randy.

"That is true," said Adnan. "The crown prince and I have been very close friends for most of our lives. I serve him as a friend and advisor, and also am in charge of his equine interests in the UAE. But I must admit, today's visit has nothing to do with horses. He requested that I meet with you today concerning the possible purchase of one of the anchor crosses that you currently have here in the CAR."

Randy got a somewhat puzzled look on his face and said, "That seems to be a very popular subject today, Adnan. Just this morning I had a meeting in which an offer was made for two of the anchor crosses."

Adnan then said with a smile on his face, "Frankly, that

doesn't really surprise me. With all the publicity the artifacts have received, along with the reported stories of how they have the power to protect their owners, I would have thought offers to purchase would be pouring into your office."

Randy laughed and said, "You are right about the publicity and the stories, but honestly the offer this morning and yours this afternoon have been the only ones presented. I think most people think that the Savior's crosses are absolutely priceless and that no amount of money could buy one. There have been several attempts to steal them, but fortunately all have failed."

Adnan then continued, "I understand. Please just allow me to present the offer from Mansour. He desired that I first made you aware of why he had an interest in the purchase. As I'm sure you know, the Sheikh and his royal family are extremely wealthy, and attempts are made frequently on them. Mansour read all the newspaper reports on all six of the anchor crosses with great interest. He thought by owning one of them he would be able to live his life without fear of anyone causing him harm. It would allow him to do so much that he presently just can't attempt because of the danger he would be putting himself in. He would, in fact, then be able to live a much more normal life. He wanted you to understand that this was the only reason he desired one of the treasures. It would simply bring peace to him. It would be used for no other purpose."

Adnan paused for a moment to allow Randy to consider what he had just said, and then he continued, "It is his understanding that each of the six anchor crosses are individually owned, and he understands that each one seems to possess the power to protect its owner. So the prince would like to ask you if you would be so kind as to make his offer known to each of the six owners. Specifically, his offer would be to pay any of the owners their asking price, and your CAR would receive an additional 10% commission from the sale."

Randy's face paled somewhat, and he then said, "A most generous offer. But as you likely know, I'm not in a position to receive or grant offers regarding the anchor crosses placed in my trust. My purpose in having them is simply to use them in my studies to try and better understand their miraculous history and power. I think my response to your offer would have to be the same as I told the other people this morning attempting to purchase two of them. We have an annual anchor cross festival coming up in the town of Harlan, Kentucky on the weekend of October 5th, only a little less than three weeks off now. I have every reason to believe that all the owners of the anchor crosses will be present at the festival. I told the people this morning that I would be pleased to present their offer to the owners at a meeting in Harlan during the festival, and I would also certainly be very pleased to present your most generous offer. My feeling is that it would be only fair for all the owners to hear both of the offers at the same time, and the fact that they all will likely be in Harlan for the festival certainly seems to be the opportunity to do this. Do you think the prince would agree to these conditions?"

Adnan said, "To me that would certainly appear to be

reasonable. But if you would permit me, I have a satellite phone and would like to give him a call to let him know what you have just offered and to find out if this would be agreeable with him."

"By all means," replied Randy. "I have a conference room next door and you would be most welcome to use it to make your call."

"Yes, thank you," said Adnan. Randy then took Adnan to the conference room and told him to take as long as he wished and then to please come back in his office to let him know the prince's decision.

Ten minutes later there was a knock on Randy's office door.

"Come in," Randy shouted.

Adnan entered, closed the door behind him, walked to the chair in front of Randy's desk, seated himself, smiled at Randy and said, "I had a good conversation with Monsour. He understood your position, and was agreeable to have you present our offer at the Harlan festival. He told me to please convey his deepest appreciation."

"That's super," Randy replied.   "This year's ACFesII is going to prove to be extremely interesting! Will either the prince, or you, or both be able to attend?"

"I think it's very likely that one or both of us will be there," said Adnan.

"Wonderful," said Randy.

"I think that concludes our business," said Adnan. "Your hospitality and cooperation are truly appreciated."

"My pleasure," replied Randy. He then stood and walked

Adan to the CAR's front door. They shook hands and Adnan departed. As Randy was walking back to his office he noticed his janitor, P. Rat Cook, talking to an Asian gentleman in the lobby. He shrugged his shoulders and continued toward his office thinking, 'This day has been one for the record book!'

As he passed Joyce he said, "If you would, I would like to talk with Dom Pelle, Felix Faure, and the Carmen sisters. I know it's late where they all live, but my guess is they are all awake and would take my call. Try and contact them one after the other. I'll try and make my conversation with each of them short." Randy then entered his office.

Just a few minutes later Joyce buzzed him and said, "Dom Pelle is on line one."

"Got it," replied Randy.

"Dom, good evening to you!" Randy said.

"And a good afternoon to you, my friend," Dom Pelle replied.

Randy then proceeded to update Dom on all the happenings. Dom Pelle was the owner of the very extensive Pelle vineyards and winery in Prato, Italy. He was the owner of the second anchor cross that Randy had found. After the briefing, Randy asked if Dom thought he might be able to attend ACFesII.

"I would not miss it!" Dom replied. "It sounds to me like it's going to be the grand finale event for the anchor crosses!"

"Those very words have been expressed," said Randy. "I will truly be looking forward to seeing you and spending some time with you. Do let me know your arrangements when you know them."

"I will indeed," said Dom. "Please give my regards to all my friends in Harlan."

"Sure will," said Randy as he hung-up the phone.

Calls followed to Felix Faure and to Elisabeth and Henriette Carmen. In addition to a plantation in the Seychelles, Felix Faure owned the Helena anchor cross. The Carmen sisters, now living in Madrid, Spain, each had inherited an anchor cross from their distant great grandfather King Louis XV of France. After being updated on all the developments, they too agreed that they did not want to miss ACFesII, and that they would start immediately to make plans to attend.

After hanging up the phone to the Carmen Sisters Randy sat back in his chair, got a huge smile on his face, and said out loud to no one in his office, "What a day this has been..... Thank you Lord!"

Chapter 8

Harlan County, Kentucky

The old bread truck pulled into the parking lot at Maggard's grocery. Fatso Chapel saw them immediately both through the front window and on his closed-circuit television monitor. Maggard's grocery was located on highway 119 about 10 miles South of Harlan, near the town of Wallins. It was operated by Trigger Green, and was really just a front for his illegal operations. Trigger was into about anything that could turn a buck. He was given the business about 15 years ago when the then owner, Pretty Boy Maggard, had 3.5 million dollars of illegal drug money found by police in two lock boxes in the Harlan Miners Bank during an attempted bank robbery. Pretty Boy managed to escape out of the country and left the business to Trigger Green. Trigger had an office in the back of the grocery. Fatso Chapel was Trigger's only employee. He took care of the grocery business, and could usually be found sitting at the check-out counter watching a small television set, reading a book or magazine, or dozing. In addition to stocking the grocery store and checking out customers, Fatso surveyed visitors to determine if they were friend or foe. Those coming to see Trigger had to go through Fatso first. If he knew them or thought they had business with Trigger he would press a button under the check-out counter that unlocked the door going into Trigger's office. Otherwise, that door remained locked. Both Fatso and Trigger had monitors that displayed what was seen by cameras positioned inside and outside their business. Fatso loved to tell corny jokes, and everyone that knew him usually would try and avoid him just to keep from having to hear one or more of his corny jokes.

The front door to Maggards opened and the two visitors entered.

"Well, well, well. As I live and breathe, I do believe Maggards is graced by the presence of Badass Brown and Bennie Sekao," Fatso proclaimed. "And what, may I ask, could I do for you?"

Badass Brown answered, "Hey Fatso, how you doin? Bennie and me got business with Trigger. Press that button and we'll head back to his office."

Badass Brown was always into some kind of crooked activity. He had over the past few years been hired several times to kill Harlan County Sheriff J. Bert Sterling. Each time he had failed, but had never been convicted due to lack of evidence. Badass was generally up to no good. His sidekick was Bennie Sekao. Bennie was Harlan's town drunk. He was usually harmless enough, although he would do most anything if rewarded by money or booze.

"Not so fast there Badass," Fatso said. "What kind of business you got with Trigger?"

Badass replied, "None of your damn business. Just press the button."

"Touchy, touchy, touchy," Fatso said. "I'll press the button just as soon as you tell me how you tell if an elephant is in your refrigerator."

"How the hell would I know?" said Badass.

"You can tell an elephant is in your refrigerator if he is wearing a sweater with an 'E' on it," said Fatso with a chuckle.

Bennie said, "That's the worst one I've ever heard you tell, Fatso."

"Press the button," demanded Badass.

Fatso complied. The two visitors walked back toward Trigger's office.

Although Trigger Green was definitely a crook, he did have a good heart. In the past few years he had passed along information to Sheriff Sterling that had likely saved his life, and on one occasion when he found out that his customer intended to assassinate the sheriff he had altered the rifle that he sold the potential assassin such that when he tried to fire it at the sheriff it exploded in his face. Sheriff Sterling, like most everyone else in Harlan County, was well aware that Trigger Green was involved in a lot of illegal activity. He just couldn't prove it. Trigger was smart.

Trigger was sitting at his desk when he noticed the visitors on one of his monitors. He saw they were coming to his office and he stood and walked around the corner of his desk to greet them. The door opened.

"Badass and Bennie, the terrible B's," Trigger said as he extended his hand to them.

"Hey Trigger," Badass said as he shook hands with Trigger. "We need to do a little business with you."

Trigger then shook hands with Bennie and said, "That's what I'm here for. Please, have a seat and let's talk."

All took a seat, and Trigger said, "Badass, I think the last time I heard anything about you was almost a year ago when apparently you tried to drop some kind of bomb from a drone onto Sheriff Sterling, and when that didn't work you tried to shoot him with a rifle."

Badass replied, "Well, all that might well have been true, but they couldn't prove it. So here I am. And I'll tell you something else, that festival is coming up again in about three weeks and I just might have a little something new for our sheriff."

Trigger then said, "You saying you going to try and take him out again?"

"I'm not here to talk about that. As I know you know, Trigger, I sell a little moonshine."

"Oh, really," said Trigger with a smile.

"Well, I got a problem," replied Badass. "Them revenuers done found my supplier's still. Tore it all to pieces. It's going to take 'em months to get up and going again. In the meantime, I got customers coming to me for shine I don't have. I know you've got a supply, so I thought maybe we could do some business."

"Could be," said Trigger. "How much you need?"

"Sort of depends on the price," said Badass, "but if we can agree on something reasonable I could use about 25 gallons."

Trigger thought a minute and then said, "I think I could handle that. I'll let you have it for $20 a gallon. You'll sell it for about $15 a quart, so that should allow you a good profit."

"So you say $500 for 25 gallons?" said Badass.

"That's what I'm saying," said Trigger.

Badass reached into his front pants pocket and pulled out a roll of bills and peeled off ten fifty dollar bills and handed them to Trigger.

"You need a receipt?" Trigger said with a chuckle.

"I just need 25 gallons of shine," replied Badass.

Trigger then looked at Bennie and said, "You gonna help him load it and then drink it?"

Bennie blushed and said, "I'll help him load it, and he might share a little with me when we get back home."

Trigger said, "Okay, you know the routine. Pull your van around back. The shine's in one gallon milk jugs in the warehouse. Fatso will go with you to unlock the warehouse and help you get all loaded."

"Damn, we gonna have to listen to more of those damnable, stinkin jokes of his," said Badass.

"Price of doing business," Trigger replied as he stood and walked to the door and opened it. "You boys take care, and

I wouldn't break any traffic laws going back home with that load of shine."

The two visitors left Trigger's office. Trigger got on his intercom and told Fatso to help them load out the 25 gallons.

"You boys ready to load a little shine?" asked Fatso when the visitors got back to the check-out counter.

"We're ready," said Bennie.

Fatso replied, "Okay, but first, tell me which elephants don't get toothaches?"

Bennie looked at Fatso with a frown and said, "I give up."

Fatso said, "The elephants that don't get toothaches are the ones that use Crest."

Badass pointed toward the door and said, "Get moving.... we've got work to do."

Fatso walked around to the warehouse in the back of the grocery store. Badass and Bennie drove the van around, and in about ten minutes they had all the moonshine loaded. Fatso locked the warehouse and said to the two as they were getting into their van, "Do you know why elephants are not in the space program?"

They got in the van and slammed the doors.

Fatso shouted to them, "Because they steal all the peanuts from the astronauts. You boys have a good day."

They drove off.

•••

Mayor Fred Knapp appeared to be the happiest man in the world! He sat at a table in Creech Cafe with Sheriff Sterling and Deputy Potter drinking coffee.

Sheriff Sterling said, "Fred, I've never seen you so happy. I guess everything coming together for the Anchor Cross Festival has put you on cloud nine."

Fred replied, "You sure got that right, Bert. Here I was all worried about them finding that final anchor cross too late for it to be in ACFesII, and now, not only will it be in the festival along with the other five, but Randy was able to get all the owners to agree to attend and participate, including high-up representatives of the Italian government. ACFesII will be a HUGE event. Our fair city will be in the news all over the world, and lots and lots of money will flow into town with all those attendees. That's certainly enough to put a giant smile on my face. Happy, happy, happy!"

"Christmas will come in October for you this year," said Kyle.

"And for all the merchants in town," replied Fred.

Fred added, "We pretty much had everything all lined up before all the news broke about the Constantine Anchor Cross. So since then we've just had to make a lot of minor adjustments to our schedule to accommodate all the owners and the new anchor cross. I think everything is looking good. The governor has cooperated tremendously in providing all the added security we need, and he's even providing a helicopter to fly all six anchor crosses from Lexington to Harlan. All that plus the great assistance from the Harlan City Police and from you guys at the sheriff's department should keep everything in line. The only thing I can think of that we haven't addressed is the weather, and I just have to leave that up to the good Lord."

Just then a little lady walked up to their table and said, "Mayor, I see you've added a new story over there on the wall." She pointed toward a clipping from the **Harlan Daily Enterprise** that Fred had taped to the wall just this morning.

"Good morning Mrs. Cavanaugh," replied Mayor Knapp. "You are certainly most observant. And you are indeed correct, I did just put that one up this morning."

"Well, I didn't mean to interrupt your meeting with Bert and Kyle, but my curiosity just got the best of me. Could you tell me the story behind it?"

Bert and Kyle both nodded and smiled at Mrs. Cavanaugh, and then Bert said, "Fred, Kyle and I would like to hear it too."

"Well, twist my arm," Fred said, and then he started. "As you notice from the picture that goes with the article, there's a fellow there holding up a can of something. As it turns out, the fellow, a Mr. Johnson, had a wife that was really cranky and critical of just about everything. Mrs. Johnson went to the grocery and got arrested by the security guard for shop lifting. When she appeared in court before Judge Oakes he asked her just exactly what she had stolen. Mrs. Johnson replied very defiantly, "Judge, it was just a stupid can of peaches." Judge Oakes then asked her why she had stolen the can of peaches. She replied, "I forgot to bring any money to the store and I didn't want to have to go back home to get the cash." Judge Oakes then asked her how many peaches were in the can. Mrs. Johnson then snarled back "Nine, but why would that matter?" Judge Oakes patiently then said, "Well Mrs. Johnson, because I'm going to give you nine days in jail, one day for each peach." As the judge was about to drop his gavel Mr. Johnson, the long suffering husband, raised his hand asking if he might speak. Judge Oakes said, "Yes Mr. Johnson, what do you wish to add?" The husband then quietly said, "Your Honor, she also stole a can of peas!"

The laughter was so loud that everyone in the restaurant stopped what they were doing to look over at Fred's table.

Bert then said, "So, I take it that the can in the guy's hand is the can of peas."

Fred replied, "Apparently so."

Kyle then asked, "Did the article say if Judge Oakes counted the peas?"

Another round of laughter followed from all four.

Chapter 9

Lexington, Kentucky

Mr. James Smith and P Rat Cook exited through the entrance doors to the University of Kentucky's Center for Appalachian Research. P Rat's shift had ended and he was headed for his car accompanied by Mr. Smith.

Mr. James Smith, aka General O, had arrived in Lexington three days ago. He, along with the five other North Koreans, had rented a seven passenger van when they flew into Atlanta, and had driven it to Lexington where they had reservations at the Hyatt. As they walked across the hotel lobby they received strange looks from those they passed. Each of the Koreans was approximately the same size, each was wearing a dark brown suit, and, of course, each looked Asian. When they arrived at the hotel reception counter they each presented their fake driver's license and credit card to the clerk. These had been prepared by North Korean government researchers using the most common United States names, as follows:

General O Kuk-mu	Mr. James Smith
Bin Yo-han	Mr. John Johnson
Choe Yong-ho	Mr. Robert Williams
General Sin Ji-hae	Mr. Michael Jones
Seo Chi-won	Mr. William Brown
Ryu Jae-gyu	Mr. David Davis

After getting settled into their hotel rooms all six spent several hours exploring the hotel and the attached shopping center (which was also appended to Rupp Arena, home to the University of Kentucky's famous basketball team). The following day General O, aka James Smith, drove to the University of Kentucky campus and found the Center for Appalachian Research. He observed carefully all day the people coming and going from the center. On the second day he returned to the CAR, entered, registered as a visitor, and toured through the accessible areas. He was not allowed to visit the museum, where the six anchor crosses were located. During his tour he noticed a janitor and approached him to make conversation. He told the janitor, P Rat Cook, that he was a salesman for Wal-Mart from China and was very interested in the anchor crosses. After the two talked for a while Mr. Smith asked Mr. Cook if he would be interested in making some money on the side. P Rat said he would, and Mr. Smith told him that he would meet him outside the CAR at the end of his shift.

The two met and walked to the parking structure where P Rat had parked his car. On their way Mr. Smith told P Rat that he would like to get into the museum to see the six anchor crosses. P Rat was about ready to tell him that wouldn't be possible when Mr. Smith said the magic words. He said, "I'm prepared to pay you ten thousand dollars cash if you can arrange for me to get in to see the anchor crosses tonight after everyone has left the Center." P Rat thought for a moment and then told Mr. Smith that he would meet him at the entrance door to the Center at midnight, and that if he had the ten thousand in cash he would take him into the museum.

P Rat arrived back at the CAR around 10 pm and told the two night guards that he and another janitor had a special cleaning job to do in the museum that night. The guards said they would be available if P Rat needed them, otherwise they would leave the two alone to do their work.

P Rat was watching for Mr. Smith. It was about 5 minutes before midnight. When P Rat spotted him walking toward the CAR he intercepted him just outside the building and pulled him over to the CAR's covered area just to the side of the entrance door. Mr. Smith had a canvas bag with the ten thousand inside it. After examining the money, P Rat handed a janitor's coverall uniform to Mr. Smith and told him to slip it on over his other clothes. He did, and the two then entered the building. P Rat ushered him to the museum, unlocked its door, and took him inside. P Rat then showed him around the museum. He told him if the guards appeared to just tell them he was working with P Rat who had gone to the bath room. P Rat then said he was leaving and told Mr. Smith to turn off all the lights when he was finished and to close the door when he left. He said the doors would lock themselves. P Rat left, and Mr. Smith was left alone in the museum.

He walked immediately to the display cases containing the six anchor crosses. As he reached to raise the cover from one of the anchor crosses he was suddenly stricken by what appeared to be a bolt of lightning. He fell to the floor, stunned unconscious. He lay without moving for about 30 minutes, and then gradually regained consciousness. He shook his head, and then stood up. Although a bit shaky, he appeared to be okay. He again stretched out his hand to raise the cover on one of the anchor cross display cases, and was again stricken by what appeared to be a bolt of lightning. He again fell to the floor....out cold. After about 45 minutes he once again regained consciousness, and then stood, although very shaky. At this point he decided that the anchor crosses were protected by some kind of invisible electrical field that would prevent him from stealing them. He decided he would have to go to plan B. He left the CAR and headed back to the Hyatt.

•••

Early the next morning General O arrived back on the University of Kentucky campus and positioned himself between the parking structure and the CAR. He waited. At 7 am P Rat exited the parking structure headed toward the CAR. General O headed to intercept him.

"Mr. Smith," P Rat said. "How did everything go last night?"

General O, aka Mr. Smith, replied, "Not well. There was some type of electrical detection device that prevented me from getting a close look at any of the anchor crosses."

"I wouldn't know about that," replied P Rat. "I'm just the janitor."

"I understand," said Mr. Smith. "I have another job for you if you would be interested in more money."

P Rat's ears perked up to the magic words and he said, "More money? I might well be interested, Mr. Smith. What do you want me to do?"

Mr. Smith replied, "From what I read in the paper, I understand that all six of the anchor crosses will be taken to a town called Harlan on the first weekend of October. Is that correct?"

"I think so," said P Rat. "About all I know about that is what's been on television and printed in the newspaper, but I think you're right."

Mr. Smith then said, "I need to know someone familiar with where the anchor crosses will be in the town called Harlan. Do you know of anyone?"

P Rat grinned and said, "Sure do. I know just the person you need to help you. How much will that be worth to you?"

"Another ten thousand dollars," replied Mr. Smith.

"You said the magic words again," said P Rat. "The person you need to be in contact with lives in a town in Eastern Kentucky called Prestonsburg. His name is Big Jim Owens.

I'll be happy to take you to meet him for the ten grand."

"That sounds good. But I'm not alone. I have five others with me. We have a rental van and are staying at the Hyatt. Can you drive your car and we'll follow you to this town called Prestonsburg?"

"Sure thing," said P Rat. "Tomorrow's Saturday, and I don't work. How about if we leave at 9 o'clock? I'll meet you in front of the Hyatt."

"That should work fine," replied Mr. Smith.

"I would need to have the ten thousand cash when we meet at the Hyatt," said P Rat. Then you would just follow me to Prestonsburg. Okay?"

"See you tomorrow morning at 9 o'clock in front of the Hyatt," said Mr. Smith.

The two shook hands. P Rat then walked to the CAR. General O walked to his car.

•••

When P Rat pulled his car into the front of the Hyatt at 9 the next morning he saw a minivan with six persons standing beside it. Each wore a brown suit. Each was about the same size, and each looked very much like Mr. Smith. It was a strange sight. He pulled in behind the minivan, placed his car in park, opened the door, got out, and walked toward Mr. Smith.

"Mr. Cook, it is good to see you this morning. Please allow me to introduce my partners," Mr. Smith said. He then started pointing down the line toward the five others. "This is Mr. Johnson, Mr. Williams, Mr. Jones, Mr. Brown, and Mr. Davis."

Each shook hands with P Rat, and he then said, "Okay, time to hit the road if you have the agreed upon compensation."

Mr. Smith then reached into the minivan and pulled out another canvas bag and handed it to P Rat, who then quickly unzipped it, looked inside, and said, "Yep, we're all set to go. Just follow me."

P Rat got in his car and pulled in front of the minivan and then out onto the road. The minivan followed closely behind.

•••

P Rat had called Big Jim last night and brought him up to date on all that had happened with Mr. Smith. He told him that he wanted to know particulars about the location of the anchor crosses during the festival in Harlan. Big Jim assured him that he knew all about where they would be, and that he would welcome Mr. Smith and his entourage to Prestonsburg. He said he'd get them motel rooms at the Dew Drop Inn, and as long as they had plenty of funds he would be able to accommodate their needs in Harlan. P Rat assured him they seemed to be flush with money. Big Jim said that was his kind of customers....bring 'em on!

After about 3 hours they pulled into the ratty gas station in Prestonsburg. Big Jim Owens and Mad Mike Hatfield were both standing outside to greet their guests. Big Jim Owens was one of Eastern Kentucky's leading drug dealers, and into most anything else illegal that would make him money. Mad Mike Hatfield was his assistant. P Rat drove in with the minivan close behind. They both parked directly in front of the dilapidated gas station. P Rat got out and shook hands with Big Jim and Mad Mike. Then the strange looking parade of six, each decked out in their brown suit and tie, emerged from the minivan and formed a line to meet Big Jim and Mike. Mr. Smith was first in line, and after meeting the two he then introduced the remaining five.

Mad Mike said, "You boys are sure dressed up."

"Ahh, Mr. Hatfield," replied Mr. Smith, "we're all salesmen and our appearance is important."

"I see," Mad Mike replied.

Big Jim then said, "Okay, we've all met. Let's go inside and talk a little business."

P Rat then said, "If it's okay with you, I'll be heading back to Lexington. I've completed my agreement with them."

This started another round of hand shaking, with all six Koreans lining up to shake P Rat's hand before he departed. He then got in his car and left for Lexington.

Everyone went to the small office in the back of the gas station. It was extremely cramped, and dirty, and started to get hot with all eight of them in the small room. All got seated.

Big Jim then said, "I understand from P Rat that you would like to do some business in Harlan. Is that correct?"

Mr. Smith spoke, "Yes. That is correct. We understand

that the six anchor crosses will be taken there for the festival on the first weekend of next month....only two weeks from now. We would like to hire you to escort us there and to point out the location of the anchor crosses. I believe I read where they would be put in a building called the Seibert Anchor Cross Memorial. Are you familiar with it?"

Big Jim said, "Oh yes, very much so. I do a lot of business in Harlan. I can certainly make arrangements for you in a motel in Harlan, and then go with you to the festival and show you the location of the Memorial building. What did you have in mind as a fee to compensate me?"

"Well, we'll be staying here in Prestonsburg until the festival. And then we'll be in Harlan for one or two nights. So I think a fee of twenty five thousand dollars should cover it," replied Mr. Smith.

"Yes, yes indeed!" Big Jim replied with a smile. "That should cover it very nicely."

Mr. Smith then reached inside his coat pocket and produced an envelope and said, "This contains fifteen thousand dollars. I will pay you the final ten thousand when we get to Harlan, if that is acceptable."

Big Jim took the envelope, looked inside, and then said, "That will work. Let's get you guys over to the Dew Drop Inn."

Chapter 10

Harlan, Kentucky

His full name was Alonzo Michael Perkins, but everyone called him "Pickem". He was 55 years old and had been born and raised in Harlan. His parents had lived in a small home in the community of Baxter, only 1 mile from the town of Harlan. Pickem was an only child, and he came along late in the lives of his parents. Both his parents had passed away, and Pickem had inherited their home. He lived there alone. He struggled but did finally complete high school. Intelligence was not his long suit. He was also lazy, and highly unmotivated. After high school he volunteered for the army, where he spent four years. After his stint in the army he came back home, lived with his parents, and did odd jobs to make a little money. After his parents died he had to find a way to make more money since he no longer had a free ride. He turned to the only thing he knew how to do well.

At an early age Alonzo Michael Perkins exhibited a very unusual skill. He possessed a natural god-given aptitude for being able to pick locks. This skill was first observed by his father when one day young Alonzo found a combination lock in his father's old tool box. The shackle on the lock had been closed, and his father had forgotten the combination required to open it. Young Alonzo played with the lock for a few minutes and his father noticed the shackle had been opened. He asked Alonzo how he did that, and Alonzo just shrugged his shoulders and said, "Don't know. I just played with it and it opened." From that day forward he had used his remarkable skill to open thousands of locks. He was particularly good at opening the ones on locked doors. During his time in the Army his skill, once discovered, was put to use by placing him on a special team having responsibilities to break into locked facilities that were owned by enemy agents. If it was a lock, Alonzo Michael Perkins could pick it. While doing this for the Army he was given the nickname "Pickem". Since he never really liked his real name, he readily accepted the new handle. To everyone who knew him in Harlan he was known as Pickem Perkins.

Although not the brightest person, Pickem realized that his remarkable skill could be used to break easily into businesses and residences to rob them. So after his parents died it was this activity Pickem pursued to provide a living. He would rob a home or business, keep any cash he found, and take any credit cards along with whatever he could conveniently carry away to sell. He would then sell this stolen merchandise usually to Trigger Green at Maggard's

Grocery. Trigger would give Pickem about ten percent of what he thought the merchandise would sell for, and would then sell it to his contacts in Knoxville, Tennessee for about half its street value. The Knoxville 'fence' would then sell the goods....usually at flea markets.

Pickem had been caught several times over the past twenty or so years, but his lawyer was always able to either get him off completely or a greatly reduced sentence. He had never spent more than about a month in jail. He was good at what he did. Sheriff J. Bert Sterling was well aware of Pickem's lock skills, but seldom had been able to gather enough evidence to convict him of his crimes.

● ● ●

Fatso saw Pickem Perkins' old beat-up panel van pull into their parking lot. The old van had been used to transport many loads of stolen goods to Maggard's Grocery.

Pickem entered the store. "Hey Fatso, you doing okay?"

Fatso replied, "Morning Pickem. You got another load of goods for us?"

"Not today," said Pickem. "I just need to discuss a little business deal with Trigger. Can you press the button to let me into his office?"

"Not a problem," replied Fatso. "But first, tell me what happened when the elephant sat on a grape."

Pickem got a frown on his face and said, "Don't know, but I bet you're getting ready to tell me."

"The grape let out a little wine," said Fatso with a chuckle as he pressed the button to allow Pickem to enter Trigger Green's office.

Trigger had been watching the exchange between Fatso and Pickem on his closed circuit television. He had stood from his desk and walked around to the door as Pickem knocked and then entered. The two shook hands and Trigger said, "Good to see you Pickem. I hope you're here for us to do a little business. Please have a seat. Can I get you a cup of coffee?"

Pickem replied, "Coffee sounds great. Just black, please."

After Trigger got coffee for the two of them he said, "Okay, what brings you to my humble little establishment today? Another load of merchandise?"

Pickem said, "Not today, Trigger. I just wanted to chat with you about an idea I have that could make us both rich."

"I'm all ears," replied Trigger.

Pickem continued, "Well, as you know this Saturday is the big festival in Harlan. From what I read in the **Enterprise** all six of those golden anchor crosses will be on display in the Memorial. Even one of them would probably be worth enough money for both of us to retire in the lap of luxury, and I couldn't even begin to imagine what all six might be worth.....maybe enough to buy a country somewhere!"

Trigger tilted his head sideways and got a curious look on his face. He then said, "You planning on trying to steal those things?"

Pickem smiled and said, "You know I'm really, really good at stealing!"

"Yeah, I know that," said Trigger, "but those things will be under heavy security when they're displayed Saturday and Sunday. I don't think you'd stand a chance of getting at them."

Pickem replied, "You're probably right about that. But what I have in mind is getting them from the sheriff's office. I figure they're stored there in his evidence room. I know they haven't said anything about them in the **Enterprise**, but I think they must have been brought in under cover and stored by the sheriff in preparation for the festival. If I'm right, they're there right now. Today's Thursday, so I'm pretty sure they would want them in place well in advance just to assure that they would be available for the weekend. So my plan is to go there around 2 a.m. tonight. As you know, the sheriff's office is only open for two shifts, and there won't be a soul there at 2 a.m. Picking the door lock and then the locks in the evidence room will be a breeze. I figure I can be in and out of there with all six of those golden anchor crosses in less than 15 minutes."

Trigger said, "So. If you're lucky enough to pull it off, what then?"

"That's why I'm here talking with you, Trigger," replied Pickem. "I need some way to fence them. I think you could do that for me. We could split the money. What'd you think?"

Trigger thought about what Pickem was proposing. He or no one else in Harlan County other than the festival planners were aware that the governor was having the six anchor crosses flown in by helicopter on Saturday morning. Trigger knew that Pickem could certainly get into the sheriff's office and the evidence room. The locks presented no problem for him. He didn't have any idea if the anchor crosses were there, but if they were there was certainly a good possibility that Pickem could deliver them.

"What you're proposing is really a major heist," Trigger said. "I would have to be ready to move them out of here immediately after you delivered them. Just as soon as the sheriff's office opened tomorrow morning they'd discover they were gone and all hell would break loose. Cops would swarm here looking for them, so I'd have to move them immediately. Probably to Knoxville. But you are right, if you could deliver them we'd both have more money than we could ever spend. Frankly, I don't see a down side to it for me. If you get caught....that's on you. If the crosses aren't there, then no one's the wiser. If you do get them and deliver them to me I'll get them to Knoxville before the sheriff's office opens tomorrow morning. In that case, we'd both head for Knoxville to broker a deal with my contact there."

"So you'll do it?" asked Pickem.

"I'll be ready," said Trigger. "I'll leave the front door to the store open and I'll be waiting for you sometime after 2 a.m. If you don't show by 3 I'll go home and go to bed and forget the whole thing, figuring you either got caught or the anchor crosses weren't there. If you show, then we're both off to Knoxville. That sound okay with you?"

"Perfect," said Pickem. "Keep your fingers crossed. I hope to see you late tonight."

The two then stood, shook hands, and Pickem left.

Trigger sat down at his desk, got out his cell phone, and placed a call to Knoxville.

On his way out of the store Fatso yelled at Pickem, "Hey Pickem, before you leave you have to tell me where an elephant would get another tail if he lost his?"

Pickem ignored Fatso and continued toward the door out of the store.

Fatso shouted, "He'd go to a retail store."

Pickem slammed the door on his way out.

● ● ●

Preacher Puss, the 15 pound long-haired gray tabby cat that lived in the sheriff's office, had just jumped down from her lofty bed located on a ledge above the entrance door and beside Deputy Potter's desk. It was her nightly routine to awaken in the middle of the night and get a snack from her food bowl, located behind the counter where Deputy Rosie Cain worked, and then return to bed to continue her night's sleep. This she had just done. She had just gotten curled up, swished her long tail a couple of times, started to purr softly, and her eyes were almost shut. Then she heard the sound. She first thought it might just be the wind blowing a branch against the building. But then she heard it again, and this time it was a little louder. It definitely seemed to be coming from the entrance door. She sat up and tilted her head slightly. Her ears were perked straight up, listening intently.

The noise continued for another couple of minutes, and then the door started to open. She got into her position to jump.

Pickem had no problem picking both the door lock and the dead bolt. It had taken him just about two minutes. He had carefully watched to make sure that no one was walking past the court house. Only cops and winos would likely be out at this hour. Fortunately, he had seen neither. Just to be on the cautious side he had brought with him his small pellet gun. He didn't own a real pistol, and didn't really want one. He could never shoot anyone. But his pellet gun looked exactly like a real pistol, and if he encountered anyone he could likely scare them with the gun, and could shoot them with a pellet as a last resort. So just in case he might encounter someone in the sheriff's office he pulled his gun as he entered. That was a very large mistake!

Preacher Puss's eyesight was remarkable, and at the moment she had her eyes open as large as silver dollars. She immediately saw a gun start through the front door, followed by an arm, and then the rest of a body. As soon as the head was through the door she pounced! Her claws were fully extended and she landed soundly on the head. The claws on each paw sank deeply into the scalp. Blood started to spurt. Her long gray hair fell all around the head, going down to about mouth level. She started screaming at the top of her lungs.

Pickem never knew what hit him. Just as he entered the office something landed on his head and he couldn't see anything. There was pain from his head like nothing he had ever encountered. Blood started to flow down his face. Whatever was on his head started to scream, and so did Pickem! He turned and started to run out of the sheriff's office.

Pickem's bad luck continued. Just as he turned and started to run down the court house steps one of the Harlan City Police patrol cars was passing directly in front of the court house, not more than 50 feet from Pickem. Their emergency lights immediately went on as they stopped their patrol car and jumped out, running to apprehend Pickem.

The city policemen yelled at Pickem to drop his pistol. They were just in the process of drawing their guns when Pickem complied and let his gun fall to the ground. When he did so, Preacher Puss jumped off his head, landed on the steps of the court house, and ran back into the sheriff's office through the still open door. She then jumped back up to her bed, curled up, swished her tail a couple of times, closed her eyes, and went to sleep.

Both police officers recognized Pickem, and it didn't take them long to figure out that he had tried to break into the sheriff's department. They also were very aware of Preacher Puss and her reputation for apprehending anyone drawing a gun in the office. They put handcuffs on Pickem and placed him in the back of their patrol car. After locking up the sheriff's entrance door, they drove Pickem to the hospital for medical care for his wounds. Pickem kept denying that he had tried to break into the sheriff's department, and said he was just walking around the court house when he was attacked by some kind of wild animal. The officers told Pickem he could tell that story to Judge Oakes. They then called Sheriff Sterling to report the break-in, and told him they would meet him at his office later in the day to report what had happened.

•••

At Maggard's Grocery Trigger Green looked at his watch. It was 3:05 a.m., and no sign of Pickem Perkins. He sighed and thought, "I've wasted a good night's sleep." He locked up the store and headed home.

Chapter 11

Harlan, Kentucky

It was Friday morning, October 4th. The Second annual Anchor Cross Festival kicked off this afternoon with limited activities. Tomorrow and Sunday were the big days. Harlan was already packed with visitors.

Mayor Fred Knapp, Sheriff J. Bert Sterling, Deputy Kyle Potter, and Dr. Randy Peters were all huddled at a table in Creech Café discussing the upcoming festival.

The mayor said, "Guys, as far as I know we've got all bases covered and everything is all set. My primary worry at the moment is the delivery tomorrow morning of the six anchor crosses. I feel sure that the governor will do everything in his power to have the helicopter safely deliver them. My understanding is that they will be picked up at 7 a.m. and then should arrive here at the helipad on the roof of the courthouse sometime between 8 and 8:30 a.m. Randy, is that your understanding?"

"Exactly," Randy replied. "I have my people all set to have the anchor crosses delivered to the UK helipad at the medical center just before 7 a.m. The governor was good enough to assign two state troopers to accompany my people to the helipad at the medical center, plus two UK police will be there too. I think it should work without a hitch."

"Excellent," Mayor Knapp said. "As you folks know, the festival will kick off at 1 p.m. today. I'll have to be there to open up the program from the stage set-up on the court house steps, and then the afternoon program will continue until around 5 p.m. Tomorrow is the big day, and we'll get everything underway at 10 a.m. I think by then we should be able to have the anchor crosses all in place in the Seibert Memorial for viewing."

Kyle Potter said, "Mayor, I know everything will come off well. Even the weather forecast is good. No sign of rain, and temperatures in the 60's. Perfect chamber of commerce weather."

"Yeah, I'm really happy about that," replied Fred. "I just want Harlan to look super for all the media coverage. It will be a big boost for our little town."

Sheriff Sterling then said, "I do have one interesting development to report to you Mr. Mayor. Kyle is aware of this, but I don't think you or Randy know about it. At around 2 a.m. this morning we had an attempted robbery at the Sheriff's Department."

Fred and Randy both stared at Bert. Fred then said, "Well, what happened?"

Bert continued, "Randy, you likely don't know Pickem Perkins, but I know the Mayor knows him well." Fred nodded his head affirmatively. "Just for Randy's information, Pickem Perkins is a local thief that has an uncanny ability to pick locks, and thus the nickname 'Pickem'. Harlan City Police Chief Asher came to my office first thing after we opened this morning to give me a report of what a couple of his men observed last night. He said that around 2 a.m. one of his patrol cars was cruising along Central Street, and when it got just about here, right in front of Creech Café and the court house, they heard a bone chilling scream coming from the direction of the court house. They were able to hear this because they had their windows down, it being such a beautiful evening and all. When they turned to look in the direction of the scream they saw a most unusual sight. They see a person, who turned out to be Pickem Perkins, running down the court house steps with blood streaming down his face and Preacher Puss perched on top his head looking for all the world like a coonskin cap.....tail and all. Pickem had what turned out to be a pellet gun in his hand. The city policemen stopped the cruiser and jumped out running toward Pickem. About that time he dropped his gun and Preacher Puss leaped to the ground and ran back into my office. The policemen arrested Pickem and took him to the hospital to get treatment for his rather extensive head lacerations."

Fred asked, "Why in the world was ole Pickem breaking into your office?"

"Don't know for sure," replied the sheriff, "but my guess would be that he thought the anchor crosses were there and he intended to steal them. Of course he denied even breaking in. He said he was just walking by the court house when some kind of wild animal attacked him."

"We'll see what Judge Oakes thinks about that story. Especially since the entrance door to the Sheriff's Department was open and Preacher Puss resides inside there," said the Mayor.

Deputy Potter laughed and said, "You're right there Mayor. Preacher Puss continues to be the least paid and best performing deputy in the department. As soon as the press gets this story her reputation will grow immensely."

All four laughed about the story and continued to drink their coffee.

Fred said, "That get-together and dinner at the Bell's last night was really something to be remembered."

"It certainly was," replied Randy. "Raymond and Betty were the perfect hosts."

All those owning and having an interest in the six anchor crosses were in Harlan by late yesterday afternoon. Randy had booked rooms for them at motels in Harlan just as soon as he knew they would be attending. The largest contingency was that for the Constantine anchor cross. In addition to Dr. Alfonso Perilli and Dr. Verla Eden representing the Italian government, the legal owner, the five members from Thomas Salvaging had also made the trip; Cooper, Clayton and Lillie Thomas from Key West, and Teagan and Jackson Lange from Ponza, Italy. Randy was able to get six rooms at the Mount

Airy motel for the 7 members representing the Constantine anchor cross. All had a private room except for Cooper and Clayton, who shared a room. Randy got Dom Pelle, owner of the Pelle anchor cross, a room at the Holiday Inn Express where he was also able to get one room shared by Elisabeth and Henriette Carmen, the twins who each owned an anchor cross. Felix Faure, owner of the Helena anchor cross accepted an invitation from Pastor Raymond and Betty Bell to stay with them. Felix and Raymond had become good friends during Raymond's time spent in the Seychelles where he discovered the Helena anchor cross in a church on the plantation owned by Felix. The first anchor cross discovered, called the Seibert, was owned by Deputy Kyle Potter who lives in Harlan. Randy was staying as a guest at the home of Sheriff J. Bert Sterling. All of the out of town guests flew into Lexington yesterday morning, rented cars, and then drove to Harlan, arriving late in the day. Pastor Raymond and Betty Bell had everyone over for a get-together and meal last evening. This morning all those that traveled into Harlan were sleeping-in to recover from their trips.

During their time together last night Randy took the opportunity to tell the anchor cross owners that they needed to meet to discuss two important and pressing issues. He refused to say further the reason for the meeting, but simply asked everyone to trust him and please agree to meet this afternoon at 3 p.m. He said the meeting would be held in city hall in the conference room. Mayor Knapp had reserved it for them. Everyone agreed.

Randy knew that both the Slusher Brothers and the crown prince of Dubai and his associate Adnan also wanted to be at the meeting. The crown prince and Adnan had rented a very nice motor home in Lexington and driven it to Harlan yesterday. Randy had talked with Sheriff Sterling about the crown prince's visit and had asked the sheriff if he could find a suitable location that might accommodate the motor home for the weekend. Bert talked with Pastor Raymond Bell about possibly letting the crown prince use a spot in the parking lot at his church. It was certainly very large and could easily accommodate the motor home. Raymond readily agreed and Bert gave all the particulars and directions back to Randy. The Slusher Brothers, living in Harlan County, did not have a concern regarding accommodations. Everything was set.

"Well, just about two more hours before show time," Mayor Knapp said. "I really think all our visitors will really enjoy ACFesII. We've got a lot of truly outstanding entertainment lined up, as well as many notable speakers. That plus getting to actually see all six of the Savior's Crosses and to hear remarks from each of the owners should give everyone something they can tell their grandchildren!"

Kyle said, "You're right Mayor. All that plus all the vendors located in the downtown area will be more than enough to keep everyone busy for the weekend."

Randy noticed a clipped newspaper article lying on the table in front of Fred. "Mayor, what's that clipping there?"

Fred replied, "Oh, that's going to be my latest addition to the wall art. Just getting ready to tape it up. Would you care to hear the story?"

The other three smiled and nodded affirmatively in unison.

Fred began, "The article is about a fellow that got to feeling really bad. His eyes were all bulged out and he had a severe ringing in his ears. He decided he had to go to his doctor to get checked out. The doctor looked him over and said he needed his tonsils removed. He agreed, but after the operation he still had popped eyes and the ringing in his ears. The man decided to consult another doctor, and the new one said he needed to have all his teeth pulled. He went to his dentist and had all his teeth extracted, but still did not feel any better. Determined to solve his problem, he went to a third doctor and after the examination the physician told the man he only had three months to live. So the man decided that he would make the most of the time he had left. He bought a flashy new car, scheduled a round-the-world cruise, and went to a tailor to get several custom-made suits. The tailor started making measurements, and when he came to the measurements for his new shirts he measured the arm length and said 34 inches and then measured the neck and said 16 inches. The man then said No, no. My neck is 15 inches, not 16. No, its 16 said the tailor. Couldn't be, said the man, I've always worn a 15. The tailor said, I'm warning you. You keep on wearing a 15 inch collar and your eyes will pop out and you'll get a ringing in your ears."

All four friends roared with laughter, and Bert said, "I bet the man started wearing a 16 inch collar."

"That would certainly be a safe bet, I'd say," replied Fred.

Bert and Kyle stood up. Bert then said, "I guess we'll head back over to the office and see if everything's quiet."

Randy joined them and said to Fred, "Thanks so much for your hospitality Mr. Mayor. I'm headed over to your conference room in city hall to get all set up for our 3 o'clock meeting."

Fred replied, "You guys are the best. I really thank you for everything. Let's keep our fingers crossed that everything goes well."

As Bert, Kyle, and Randy reached the door to exit they heard Polly squawk, "Bye, bye boys. Bye, bye boys."

Each reached up to Polly's perch and gave the bird a good stroke as they left Creech Café.

Chapter 12

Pineville, Kentucky

ig Jim Owens and Mad Mike Hatfield pulled their car into the parking lot at the Pine Mountain State Resort Park located just outside Pineville, Kentucky, which is about 35 miles from Harlan. Following behind Big Jim's car was the minivan driven by General O, aka Mr. James Smith, along with his five comrades. Big Jim had tried to get motel accommodations for the group in Harlan, but everything was sold out. When he started checking other towns reasonably close to Harlan he lucked upon being able to get the last four lodge rooms available at the Pine Mountain State Park. The reservations were for two nights, tonight (Friday) and tomorrow night. Mr. Smith had told Big Jim that they wanted to be able to view the anchor crosses in the Memorial on Saturday afternoon, and then return to the state park to spend Saturday evening. They would depart their separate ways on Sunday morning. The plan was to depart for Harlan early tomorrow morning. Big Jim knew the town would be very crowded, and had called Trigger Green and made arrangements for Fatso and one of his friends to drive them from Maggard's Grocery to Harlan, drop them off, and then return to pick them up at 4 p.m. Trigger demanded $500 for this taxi service. Big Jim told him that was robbery, but finally agreed to the fee. After checking into the lodge everyone enjoyed the food in their restaurant and hiking the beautiful trails around the park.

At midnight General O pulled out his satellite phone and made his nightly call to Kim Jong-un to brief him on the day's activities. Kim was pleased with the report. He told General O that after they had the six anchor crosses in their possession to follow through with their plans with Big Jim and return to the state park for the evening. When General O called him on Saturday night he would give them their orders. Kim had not told the General what his intentions were, but he had formulated a plan wherein the six soldiers would drive to Washington, D.C. and then use the protection of the anchor crosses to gain control of the White House. From there he had a long list of demands that the U.S. would have to comply with, all of which would vastly enrich Kim and his North Korean government. Kim was getting very excited. So much so that he celebrated with a lunch of four Big Macs, three orders of french fries, and two chocolate milk shakes.

•••

Harlan, Kentucky

At precisely 1 o'clock Mayor Fred Knapp rose from his chair on the stage and walked to the microphone at the podium. "Good afternoon ladies and gentlemen. My name is Fred Knapp, Mayor of Harlan, and I'm here to welcome each of you to the start of our second annual anchor cross festival. The good Lord has blessed us with wonderful weather, and the hard working program committee has blessed us with a great lineup of outstanding entertainment and speakers this year. I know many of you are here particularly to see the beautiful anchor crosses, and especially to see the final one, the Constantine Anchor Cross. I'm pleased to say that not only will all six of the magnificent artifacts be on display starting tomorrow at 10 a.m. in the Seibert Anchor Cross Memorial building right over there," and he pointed toward the Memorial located in the northwest corner of the court house property, just about 100 feet from where he was standing, "But we are also tremendously honored to have with us this year the owners of each of the anchor crosses. They will be with us tomorrow starting at 10 o'clock right here on the main stage. Each will offer comments and hopefully be available to take any questions you might have."

Fred went on to introduce each of the ACFes program committee and then went over the program details for Friday afternoon. ACFessII was off and running.

•••

Dr. Randy Peters had gone from the meeting at Creech Café directly to the conference room at city hall, located only a couple of blocks south of the court house. The Mayor had reserved several parking spaces at city hall for those coming to attend the 3 o'clock meeting. Randy wanted to arrange the chairs and tables to accommodate the 19 people he was expecting for the meeting. Also, he had asked Pastor Raymond Bell to meet him at about 1:30 to discuss the meeting agenda.

It was about 1:30 and Randy was sitting in a chair at the end of the table thinking about exactly what could be accomplished from the upcoming meeting. He was deep in thought when he heard, "Hey Randy, am I early?" It was Pastor Raymond Bell.

"No, no, not at all, Raymond. Please, come in and have a seat. We need to talk."

Raymond pulled up a chair across the table from Randy and sat. He then said, "Okay my friend, I'm all ears!"

Randy began, "Raymond, let me first thank you sincerely for volunteering to help me with this meeting. I don't think I could have done it alone. I know you will recall the conversation you and I had last night at your home regarding the two offers to purchase anchor crosses." Randy had briefed Raymond in confidence last evening on the offers from the Crown Prince of Dubai and the Slusher Brothers.

"Oh yes indeed," replied Raymond. "That has been on my mind almost constantly since you shared the information with me."

Randy continued, "Well, as we discussed, these two offers are on the table, so to speak, and both parties making the offers will be here for our 3 o'clock meeting, in addition to all the anchor cross owners. My thought is that we should initially exclude the potential purchasers from the meeting so that we might first explain their offers to the owners. I can do that. But after that I would like for you to share your heart-felt thoughts about whether or not the owners should consider selling. What you would care to say is entirely up to you. I feel certain you have given this both thought and prayer. These artifacts are absolutely unique and priceless. They possess some kind of supernatural power, and certainly I think that it is somehow related to the fact that our Lord Jesus Christ blessed the gold from which they are made. I'll stop here and simply ask if you would be willing to do this?"

"You know the answer to that," Pastor Bell replied. "Of course I will. I have indeed given the matter thought and prayer, and do have thoughts that I would be pleased to share. You just need to understand that what I have to say simply represents my own personal opinion. It could certainly be right or wrong."

"I appreciate that," Randy said. "I just think that you are in the best position to talk with the owners about the ramifications of selling. I do indeed greatly appreciate your willingness to do this."

"It is my pleasure, my friend," replied Raymond. "But I would appreciate it if you would now give the hour or so before the start of the meeting to put together some thoughts and notes. Also, a nice cup of coffee would be welcome."

"Good on both requests," Randy replied. "How about if you use the mayor's office? That's where I propose to sequester the proposed buyers during our meeting with the owners. After our meeting I'll ask the proposed buyers to join us and we can introduce them and explain to them what was decided in our meeting. Does that sound okay?"

"I think that would work well.....don't forget my coffee," Raymond said as he walked from the conference room into the mayor's office with a notepad.

Randy walked to the city hall's office to grab two cups of coffee.

•••

Deputy Kyle Potter was the next to appear for the meeting. Randy had asked Kyle to pick up the crown prince and his associate, Adnan, from their motor home parked in the lot at Pastor Raymond Bell's New Hope Baptist Church. Kyle was very curious about why the crown prince of Dubai would be attending their meeting, but Randy just told him he'd have to wait to find out. Upon their arrival Randy ushered them into the mayor's office, which had been vacated by Pastor Bell, and explained to them that they would be joined by the Slusher Brothers shortly and to please just enjoy chatting until the anchor cross owner's meeting was finished. They agreed.

Just a couple of minutes later Gunsmoke and Booger Slusher arrived with their financial advisor, Mr. August J. Richenberger. Randy explained to them that the owners were going to first meet, after which the potential buyers would join them, and requested that they join the crown prince and Adnan in the mayor's office until called. They agreed.

Each of the owners then arrived. The largest delegation by far was that representing the Constantine Anchor Cross. Seven total in number, including the two from the Italian government and five from Thomas Salvaging. The Carmen Sisters, Dom Pelle, Felix Faure, and Kyle Potter completed the owners. Each took a seat at the conference table, along with Pastor Bell and Randy Peters. Randy had made both coffee and soft drinks available in both the conference room and in the mayor's office. Each at the conference table selected a beverage and started to chat with those around them.

Randy stood up and said, "If I could have your attention we'll get our meeting underway. First of all I would like to thank each of you for agreeing to meet this afternoon, especially so since I wouldn't tell you the purpose of the meeting. But you are now about to find out. Waiting in the mayor's office are two parties that have a desire to purchase an anchor cross. I have met with each of these and have heard their stories as to why they would like to own one of the Savior's Crosses. Their reasons are very sound. One party consists of two brothers who live here in Harlan County. They are the Slusher Brothers, are quite wealthy, and would like to purchase two anchor crosses, one for each of them, for 25 million dollars each. They have stated that they desire the anchor crosses solely for protection. Because of their immense wealth they have constant concerns for their safety. They have their financial advisor, Mr. August J. Richenberger, accompanying them today. The other party is the crown prince of Dubai from the United Arab Emirates, Sheikh Mansour bin Ahmed Al Maktoum. His reason for wanting to purchase an anchor cross is similar to that of the Slusher Brothers. He wishes it solely for protection. As I'm sure you are well aware, he is wealthy beyond measure. He is accompanied today by his long time trusted friend Adnan bin Saeed Al Amin. The crown prince says he is prepared to pay the asking price for one anchor cross. In all fairness, I must also tell you that the Slusher Brothers donated one million dollars to my Center for Appalachian Research, without any strings attached. They only asked that I present their offer to you. The crown prince said that he would also pay my center 10% of whatever price he might pay for an anchor cross. I tell you this only so you will be aware of all the financial arrangements. I certainly do not endorse either offer. I am just presenting the offers for your consideration. It is entirely up to you to decide if you would like to sell your anchor cross. With that, I'm going to sit down and ask Pastor Raymond Bell to share his thoughts with you. After Raymond finishes, we'll entertain questions and then ask the two potential buyers to join us. Raymond."

Raymond stood and said, "Thanks Randy. I do have just a few thoughts to share with you as you consider selling your anchor crosses. Firstly, I would like to say that as far as I know there has been not a single reported instance of where someone was protected while wearing an anchor cross for the purpose of protection. As you are all well aware, and in fact I think each of you has personally experienced, the anchor crosses do have an astounding capability to protect those that wear them so long as the outcome supports a peaceful purpose. The proposed buyers want to purchase anchor crosses for the specific purpose of continually being provided protection by them. Whether or not they would do this is certainly a question. Always in the past when their power was exhibited it was simply as a consequence of the anchor cross being worn, not that it was being worn for the purpose of protection. So, the point is, we really don't know if the anchor crosses would provide protection if worn for that purpose. They might, but we truly don't know. Frankly, we really don't know very much at all about their mysterious powers. So to sell one for the express purpose of providing protection for the person wearing it could well prove to be unwise, and could possibly even result in their death or serious injury. Bottom line, we just don't know. The other thought I wanted to share with you relates to their religious aspect. We know that the gold from which the crosses were cast by Constantine had been passed down through the church after having been blessed by our Lord Jesus Christ and then given to St. Peter to help start the church. Whether or not this blessing is somehow associated with the mysterious powers exhibited by the anchor crosses is another question that remains unanswered. It certainly would seem possible, but we just don't know. Further, we don't know whether or not the anchor crosses are capable of other miraculous deeds. For example, might it be possible under certain conditions that when one or more of them are placed in some kind of controlled environment they might provide information regarding their past, or perhaps might somehow give a sign of something to come in the future? We don't know. Again, we really don't know much about them at all. And this brings me to the point where I'm going to make a suggestion. Please keep in mind that it is just a suggestion. Also, I want to be very clear that I have not discussed this at all with Randy. It is purely my own suggestion. And it is this: Since we clearly know so little about the Savior's Crosses, why not keep them all together and allow Randy to pursue his research on them in an attempt to unlock some of their mysteries. Please note that my suggestion is that all six of them be retained by Randy for study. The reason I say this is just on the chance that maybe all six together could provide answers that were not possible with five or less. There could be something that manifests itself from the presence of all six of the artifacts that would not be detected if fewer were present. All this is speculation. But I think that each of you, having experienced the amazing, mysterious, and powerful force associated with these anchor crosses, would like to better understand them, and learn their capabilities and limitations. And I would submit that this could only be established if they all remain with Dr. Peters for his research and study. That's my spiel. And do please understand that I will not be offended in the least if one or more of you decide you would like to sell. That's your decision. I appreciate your listening to me."

Raymond took a seat, and Randy again stood and said, "Raymond, I must say that was totally unexpected. I will hasten to say that I certainly don't disagree with you, but like you I would certainly understand if one or more of you owners decide to sell. It's totally up to you. I think the floor is open for comments."

Elisabeth Carmen put up her hand to be acknowledged. Randy said, "Yes Elisabeth, please go right ahead."

"Thank you Dr. Peters," Elisabeth said. "I can only speak for myself, although I feel it extremely likely that my sister Henriette will also agree with me. I have absolutely no interest in selling my anchor cross at any price." Henriette Carmen nodded approvingly. "Pastor Bell's proposal to leave them at the CAR for research has great merit, and that's exactly what I intend to do."

Kyle Potter raised his hand to speak. Randy replied, "Yes Kyle, please speak."

Kyle said, "Thanks Randy, and thanks to Elisabeth Carmen. Her thoughts are my thoughts. I think I'm the only owner that is not wealthy. Certainly the good Lord has greatly blessed me in many, many ways. But the accumulation of great wealth is not one of them. So to be presented with the possibility of selling my Seibert Anchor Cross for untold millions of dollars is certainly tempting. But I truly believe everything Pastor Bell just said about the need for more research to try to better establish and understand the powers that apparently somehow reside in these golden anchor crosses. I currently enjoy my job very much. It is fulfilling to me, and I certainly have enough money for all my needs. So I'll go along with the

Carmen sisters and leave the Seibert Anchor Cross at the CAR for further study."

Dom Pelle next held up his hand to be acknowledged. Randy said, "Mr. Dom Pelle, please speak."

"Thank you very much Dr. Peters," Dom said. "I must say, the wine business has been very good in Italy this year," lots of laughter was heard from all at the table, "so I think I'll just go along with the Carmen Sisters and Deputy Potter and leave the Pelle Anchor Cross at the CAR for Dr. Peters' research. Who knows, he might find a way they can double the output of my vineyards!" More laughter came from those at the table.

The next hand to go up was from Felix Faure, owner of the Helena Anchor Cross. Randy said, "Yes Mr. Felix Faure, the floor is yours!"

"I certainly would not want to imply that I couldn't use a few hundred million dollars," replied Felix as everyone gave another chuckle, "but I will have to admit that I think it far more important that Dr. Peters be allowed to keep my Helena Anchor Cross for his study than for me to stuff my bank account. Everything said by Pastor Raymond Bell rings true. I'll leave my Savior's Cross at the CAR for the time being."

"Thanks Felix, appreciate those comments," said Randy as he looked toward the Constantine Anchor Cross delegation. Dr. Alfonso Perilli looked at Dr. Verla Eden. They both smiled, and Dr. Perilli raised his hand to speak.

"Thank you Dr. Peters," Dr. Perilli said. "Dr. Eden and I sort of thought this meeting might well be about one or more offers to purchase. So we have discussed it. And just as long as you can assure me that word will not get back to the Italian government about the very generous offers, we have definitely decided that we will not sell the Constantine Anchor Cross. We agree totally with Pastor Bell's comments. We think there are many more discoveries to be made regarding the Savior's Crosses, and these will only be established through a thorough research program. Dr. Peters and his center are uniquely qualified to continue their research and study, and the Italian government will leave the Constantine Anchor Cross at the CAR for that purpose."

Dr. Perilli then looked straight at the 5 members of the Thomas Salvaging Company that sat at the conference table with inquisitive looks on their faces and said, "I know that my good friends from Thomas Salvaging are wondering about their share in the Constantine Anchor Cross. Without their finding it, we wouldn't be here today. I want to use this opportunity to announce to them that the Italian government has agreed to pay them 25 million dollars for salvaging the Constantine Anchor Cross." There was a loud round of applause from all those at the table.

The Thomases and the Langes looked to be in shock. Huge smiles slowly began to form on their faces. Handshakes and backslaps followed. Cooper Thomas then said, "Dr. Perilli and Dr. Eden, on behalf of all five of us I want to thank you from the bottom of our hearts. Not only can we really, really use the money, but we are so pleased to know that the Constantine Anchor Cross will remain in Dr. Peters' research study. We feel certain great things will be forthcoming from that program. Thank you so very much!"

Randy then said, "Okay. It looks like we've accomplished our purpose for this meeting. In just a moment I'll invite our two potential buyers in to hear what you've decided."

Randy then continued to discuss exactly what they would say to the crown prince and to the Slusher brothers, and then he walked to the door to the mayor's office, opened it, and invited the five persons to join everyone in the conference room.

Five chairs had been arranged at one end of the conference room table to accommodate the potential buyers. The other 13 were seated along the sides of the table, and Randy stood at the other table end. He spoke, "Friends, I would like to introduce to you our guests having an interest in purchasing one or more of the anchor crosses. I'll go from left to right at the other end of the table. First we have the crown prince of Dubai, Sheikh Mansour bin Ahmed Al Maktoum and his associate Adnan bin Saeed Al Amin. Next are the Slusher Brothers, Gunsmoke and Booger, and their financial advisor, Mr. August J. Richenberger." Each smiled and nodded as they were introduced. Randy then asked each of the other 13 seated at the table to introduce themselves to their visitors, which they did.

After the introductions Randy said, "As I'm sure you are aware, we just concluded a meeting devoted entirely to your generous offers to purchase anchor crosses. After a full discussion there was a unanimous agreement. The decision reached by the owners was to keep all six of the anchor crosses at the Center for Appalachian Research for further study and evaluation." He then proceeded to give a condensed version of Pastor Bell's presentation, after which he said, "So, those were the primary reasons the owners decided to retain their anchor crosses. They each appreciate very much your interest in purchasing them, and have indicated that if at some time in the future they decide to sell you would have the first opportunity to purchase. In the meantime, they will remain at the CAR."

The crown prince raised his hand. He was dressed in jeans and a sport shirt, as was his friend Adnan. Randy said, "Yes, please speak."

The crown prince said, "My friends, it is a great honor for me and Adnan to be here with you. We have experienced wonderful hospitality from everyone we've met. Please call us Monsour and Adnan. I respect your decision. It was not unexpected. I appreciate how very special the artifacts are, and do understand that more research is needed to discover their full potential. I must frankly admit to being a bit disappointed not to have one of them, but do appreciate your offer to purchase if and when one might be available for sale. Adnan and I frequently travel to Lexington to attend the Keeneland horse sales, and we will certainly keep in touch with Dr. Peters and his research program. I hope he won't mind us dropping by when we're in Lexington."

Randy replied, "Monsour, it will always be a great pleasure to have you and Adnan as guests at the CAR. Please always put us on your schedule when in Lexington."

August J. Richenberger then held up his hand to speak. Randy responded, "Yes Gus, please speak."

Gus said, "I think you are all aware that I am the financial advisor for the Slusher brothers. Like Monsour, the brothers and I have previously discussed the possibility that you would not want to sell at this time. Also like Monsour, we are disappointed, but do understand. We appreciate your consideration, and also your offer to contact us first if anchor crosses become available for sale in the future."

Gunsmoke Slusher then held up his hand. Randy said, "Yes Gunsmoke."

"Booger and I aren't real good at talking," responded Gunsmoke, "but we ain't dumb. What Gus said is true, and I just wanted to thank each of you for your consideration."

A big round of applause followed.

Randy then said, "Well, I think we've come to the end of our meeting. It was very productive, and I appreciate so much each of you being here and thank you for participating. Please feel free to spend a little more time chatting with our visitors, and then I hope that you will all enjoy the activities of our second annual Anchor Cross Festival.

Chapter 13

Harlan, Kentucky

Thwap-thwap-thwap-thwap. A big smile formed on the faces of Mayor Knapp and Dr. Peters as they heard the approaching helicopter. They stood on the roof of the Harlan County Court House, beside its helipad. It was 8:15 on Saturday morning. They heard the aircraft before they could see it. Now they could clearly see it approaching from the north. Along with Sheriff Sterling and Deputy Potter they ducked back into the shelter of the roof access to get out of the helicopter's downwash. All four watched as the chopper sat down gently on the helipad. Its rotors then started to slow to a stop.

The greeting party of four then came out of the shelter and approached the helipad. The chopper's door opened and out stepped Kentucky's governor Brad Shear along with State trooper Ape Cornett. Ape was originally from Harlan, and had served as Sheriff Sterling's chief deputy prior to deciding to pursue a career with the state police. It was his position that Kyle Potter filled. Kyle and Ape were good friends. Trooper Cornett carried an impressive looking box.

Mayor Knapp stepped forward with his hand extended to Governor Shear and said, "Well, well. What a pleasant surprise! We didn't get any advance notice of your joining us today, governor. Thank you so much for coming!"

"Wouldn't miss it for the world," the governor replied. "I took the liberty of hopping on the helicopter with Trooper Cornett. I knew Ape was from Harlan and would enjoy the weekend duty here. I think you'll find all six of the anchor crosses in that box he's carrying. I'll tell you one thing.....we certainly felt completely safe on our trip," the governor said with a big grin.

Deputy Ape Cornett shifted the box to his left arm and shook hands with Dr. Peters. He then handed him the box and shook hands with Fred and Bert. He and Kyle embraced and patted each other on the back. The governor greeted the other three and chatted briefly with them. All then departed back into the court house to prepare for the ceremony at 10 a.m.

●●●

Fatso was expecting the two vehicles as they pulled into Maggard's Grocery's parking lot. Trigger had asked Fatso to get his cousin Whalebait Chappel to drive one of the vehicles and for him to drive the other. Fatso and Whalebait watched as Big Jim Owens got out of his car and started walking into the grocery.

Fatso and Whalebait were standing behind the counter at the grocery's checkout. Big Jim walked in the door and said, "Hey Fatso, I see you got your cousin Whalebait there. He going to drive one of the cars?"

Fatso responded, "Yeah. That's what Trigger told us."

"I guess I need to see him," said Big Jim. "How about pressing that button for his office."

"Sure thing, Big Jim," replied Fatso. "But first you gotta tell me why elephants drink so much."

Big Jim just kept walking toward the door to Triggers office.

"Because they have so much to forget!" Fatso said with a chuckle as he pushed the button to unlock the door to Trigger's office.

Trigger was standing at his desk as Big Jim came in. He said, "Well, well, the Prestonsburg Flash."

"Hey Trigger, Fatso's driving me crazy with those dumb jokes. Everything all set for him and Whalebait to drive us?"

"Will be just as soon as you grease my palm with $500," replied Trigger.

Big Jim reached in his pocket and removed a wad of bills, peeled off ten fifties and handed them to Trigger. He then said, "Now are we all set?"

"Money talks," replied Trigger. "As I understand it Fatso and Whalebait will drive your two cars to the festival, let everyone out, and then come back to pick you up at the same spot at 4 p.m. Those are the orders I gave them. Correct?"

"Yeah, that's it," replied Big Jim. "Just one more thing. I sure as hell don't want to be in the same car with Fatso and have to listen to those damn corny jokes. You tell Whalebait to drive my car and let the others have to listen to Fatso."

"I can do that," replied Trigger as he came around his desk and walked with Big Jim back into the grocery store. Big Jim headed to his car. Trigger walked over to the checkout counter and said, "Whalebait, you drive Big Jim's car and Fatso will take the minivan." Trigger then removed the ten fifties from his pocket and peeled off two and handed them to Whalebait and then two more and handed those to Fatso. He kept the remaining $300.

Fatso and Whalebait smiled big as they looked at the money, and then started walking out of the store. Trigger walked around the counter and sat down at checkout. He then yelled at the two as they were going out the door, "You boys drive safely.....see you back here shortly."

Big Jim and Mad Mike were standing outside their car. As Whalebait and Fatso approached Big Jim walked to the minivan and slid open the side door. Fatso walked beside Big Jim and said, "I understand I'm to drive this one."

"That's right, Fatso," replied Big Jim. "These gentlemen are salesmen. You are to treat them well. You just follow my car, and we'll expect you two back with the cars to pick us up at 4 o'clock at the same spot where you drop us off....got it?"

"Got it," said Fatso as he slid under the wheel in the driver's seat of the minivan. As Trigger started to walk back to his car Fatso yelled, "Hey Big Jim. You know the best way to keep fish from smelling?"

Big Jim continued walking. Fatso shouted, "You cut off their noses!"

Big Jim got in the front passenger seat of his car. Whalebait was in the driver's seat and Mad Mike had gotten in the back seat. Big Jim said to Whalebait, "Your cousin's driving me crazy with those damnable jokes. I feel sorry for my associates in the minivan. Pull around them and they'll follow you to Harlan. I'll tell you where to drop us off."

The two cars left Maggard's Grocery.

About half an hour later they arrived at the corner of Mound and Main streets in Harlan. The drive would normally have taken only about half as long, but the traffic was heavy due to the festival. The two vehicles pulled into the parking lot in front of the Harlan Baptist Church. It was only a short walk from there to the Court House. Big Jim and Mad Mike got out of their car and looked at the minivan. What they saw shocked them. The six passengers were getting out, one after the other with huge smiles on their faces. Fatso had gotten out first, and as each of his passengers emerged they shook hands vigorously with him and slapped him on his back. Two of the six were doubled over laughing. Two more were holding their sides as they laughed uncontrollably. Fatso then said, "Just one more. If a person crosses the ocean twice without taking a bath what do you call him?" All six looked at Fatso with wide, anticipating eyes.

"You call him a dirty double crosser," Fatso replied with a laugh. All six immediately started clapping their hands and doubled over laughing. Tears poured from their eyes.

Fatso then shook hands with each of them and said he would see them at 4 o'clock.

General O, aka James Smith, said, "Thank you so much Mr. Fatso. We all enjoyed our ride with you greatly and will look forward to seeing you again at 4 o'clock."

"No problem," replied Fatso.

"Follow me," shouted Big Jim. He and Mad Mike walked side by side down Main Street toward Central Street, where they would turn left to walk another couple of blocks to the Court House. Following immediately behind them were the six North Koreans in a line, each wearing a suit. It was a most unusual looking procession.

•••

It was just a few minutes before 10 a.m. The stage built on the steps of the court house was crowded. A crowd estimated at several thousand had gathered in front of the court house, extending up and down Central Street. An excellent audio system had been set up so that all could easily hear everything from the stage. Media personnel occupied the front row beside the stage. Video cameras had been set up on tripods and many reporters carried their own hand held cameras. The podium on the stage had at least 20 different microphones attached by the media. The October sun blazed down. The temperature was 63 degrees....perfect weather.

The six anchor cross owners sat in chairs on the stage. Sheriff Sterling stood at one end of the stage along with two

Kentucky state troopers. Three additional state troopers stood on the other end of the stage. Mayor Knapp, Dr. Randy Peters, and Governor Shear were seated beside the anchor cross owners. A musical group had just vacated the stage, and all now awaited the start of the ceremony.

Sheriff Sterling looked out at the huge audience and noticed Big Jim Owens and Mad Mike Hatfield from Prestonsburg pushing their way through the crowd on Central Street. Immediately behind them was a line of six rather short individuals, each wearing a dark brown suit. All six appeared to be Asian and looked very much out of place in Harlan. Knowing Owens and Hatfield, Bert wondered if the group was going to be trouble. He punched Deputy Kyle Potter, sitting beside him, and pointed out the procession. Kyle nodded in acknowledgement. He too knew the two crooks and immediately was on alert. Bert and Kyle then noticed that the eight of them stopped and just stood watching the stage.

At exactly 10 a.m. Mayor Knapp walked to the podium and greeted the crowd. After introducing everyone on the stage he invited Governor Shear to offer comments, which he did.

Mayor Knapp then asked Dr. Randy Peters to discuss his involvement with the anchor crosses. Randy shared his involvement and research with all six artifacts, and wound up his comments by saying that all the anchor cross owners had agreed to allow the Center for Appalachian Research to retain the artifacts for additional study and research. The six anchor cross owners, each wearing his or her anchor cross, were then asked to make comments.

The first was Deputy Kyle Potter, wearing the Seibert anchor cross. After thanking everyone for attending, he briefly related his finding the first of the anchor crosses. Kyle had told his story to many church, civic, and school groups, and it was eagerly received by today's ACFesII audience.

Next up was Dom Pelle, owner of the Pelle anchor cross. Dom related how Randy Peters had visited the church in Prato, Italy where the Pelle anchor cross was on display, and how on their flight back to the U.S. the artifact had saved their lives as well as those of the hundreds of other passengers. He expressed his sincere thanks to everyone in Harlan for being so hospitable to him during his visits here. He concluded his remarks by talking about how well the vineyard of Jan and Jake Keller was developing. Several years ago Dom visited Harlan and participated in a ceremony that featured his Pelle anchor cross. During that visit he happened to drink some wine made by the Keller's on their small farm near Wallins, in Harlan County. The wine was excellent, and proved to be equal to that produced from the Pelle vineyards in Prato, Italy. Dom thought growing grapes and producing wine could be an excellent boost to the economy of Harlan County. He found 100 acres of suitable land, purchased it, and talked Jan and Jake Keller into managing it. All was on track with his Harlan County vineyard.

Felix Faure, owner of the Helena anchor cross, spoke next. He talked about the visit of Pastor Raymond Bell to his plantation in the Seychelles archipelago and how the

Helena anchor cross had been discovered in a small chapel. He further discussed the history of his artifact, and the crowd listened intently as he told how the one side of his Savior's Cross was made from wood thought to be from the actual cross upon which Jesus Christ was crucified, and how in 326 A.D. Helena had traveled from Rome to Jerusalem wearing the golden anchor cross.

The Carmen Sisters were next up. Elisabeth Carmen spoke first and told the history behind the anchor crosses that she and her sister Henriette owned. She described how they had been given to King Louis XV of France and then passed down through the royal family to them. She then introduced her sister.

Henriette told several stories about how their anchor crosses had mysteriously saved the two of them from harm, and then thanked everyone for their wonderful visit to Harlan.

The final speaker representing those owning the anchor crosses was Jackson Lange. Although not really the owner, Drs. Perilli and Eden insisted that Jackson wear the Constantine anchor cross and tell the story of how he and Teagan had found it. Jackson was not accustomed to talking to large audiences, but his sincere appreciation for the artifact and the generosity of the Italian government enabled his talk to be extremely well received.

At the conclusion of the comments from the owners, Mayor Knapp asked all six to please stand in a line across the front of the stage so that the media could get video footage and photographs of them all together wearing their magnificent golden anchor crosses. This they did. For the next fifteen minutes pictures and videos were taken which would be seen all around the world after the reporters filed their stories. The mayor then said questions would be entertained. Several portable microphones were passed to those in the audience raising their hands with questions. The Q&A session lasted another 30 minutes.

Mayor Knapp then reviewed the schedule for the rest of Saturday and for Sunday. He announced that all six of the anchor crosses would be taken immediately to the Seibert Memorial and would be on display there starting at 1 p.m. He then declared the morning session adjourned.

Sheriff Sterling watched closely the group that was with Big Jim Owens. At adjournment of the morning session he saw the eight of them walk to a street vendor and purchase some food for lunch. They all grabbed a table and sat to eat their food. Bert then joined with the five state troopers to accompany the owners to the Seibert Memorial. One officer accompanied each owner. They proceeded immediately to the memorial and placed their anchor crosses in special, secure display cases that had excellent lighting and each had a rotating pedestal upon which the anchor cross was placed. The five state troopers that accompanied the owners stayed in the memorial to guard the artifacts. Bert then left with Kyle to go to Creech Café for lunch. Everything seemed under control.

As they walked up Central Street toward Creech Café they passed the vendor with the table where Big Jim and his delegation were seated having lunch. Bert walked over to

Big Jim and said, "Looks like our little festival has drawn some visitors from Prestonsburg."

Big Jim looked at Bert and replied, "Howdy sheriff. Yes indeed, and quite a show it is! I think you know my associate here, Mr. Hatfield, and these other gentlemen are salesmen from China."

"I James Smith, salesman. I John Johnson, salesman, I Robert Williams, salesman, I Michael Jones, salesman. I William Brown, salesman, I David Davis, salesman," each of the six replied.

Bert shook hands with each of them and said, "Gentlemen, it's a pleasure to have you as visitors here in Harlan for our festival. This is my deputy, Kyle Potter," Kyle tipped his hat to them and smiled, "Enjoy your stay in our little town."

"See you sheriff," Big Jim said as he took another huge bite from his cheeseburger. The six North Koreans waved bye.

Bert and Kyle proceeded to walk toward Creech Café for lunch. Kyle said, "Something strange about that group."

Bert replied, "Yeah, sure is, but they're well behaved and not breaking any of our laws. Let's just keep an eye on 'em."

Chapter 14

Harlan, Kentucky

Bert and Kyle finished lunch and walked back to the Seibert Anchor Cross Memorial building. On their way they noticed that Big Jim and his visitors were still seated at the table, now apparently enjoying desserts.

Upon arrival at the Memorial Bert noticed that two Kentucky State Troopers were stationed just outside the entrance with a metal detector set up to screen visitors before they entered the building. He and Kyle spoke to the two troopers and then entered the building. It was about 12:30 p.m. Inside, the six golden anchor crosses were prominently displayed in their cases. Standing behind each anchor cross was its owner (Jackson Lange stood behind the Constantine anchor cross as requested by Dr. Perilli, representing the Italian government). Deputy Kyle Potter walked behind the display case containing the Seibert anchor cross. Bert was pleased to see that in addition to Kyle there were five other law enforcement officers in the Memorial. These five stood along the wall on the opposite side from where the anchor crosses were displayed. Thus when the visitors entered the Memorial they would pass between the troopers on their left and the display cases on their right.

It had been decided that groups of 25 people would be allowed in for viewing the anchor crosses. One of the troopers at the metal detector would keep count and allow 25 to enter. The entrance door would then be closed, and the 25 would be allowed exactly five minutes to view the artifacts. The state troopers inside the memorial would time them, and after five minutes the one closest to the back door would walk to it, open it, and announce that time was up and would the visitors please begin to exit. The additional time required for the 25 to enter and exit was about five minutes. So all together the cycle time was about ten minutes for each group of 25.

By 1 p.m. the line in front of the Memorial had grown to several hundred. It stretched from the front of the Memorial all the way down the western side of the court house property along 1st Street and then it turned behind the court house and ran almost to 2nd Street. Big Jim and his group remained at their table and watched the Memorial. They had a good view of the back door, but couldn't see the entrance. At exactly 1 o'clock 25 people were admitted through the metal detectors. After a few minutes the back door opened and Big Jim looked at his watch. He also counted the number of people that came out. He then waited until the back door opened again, and looked at his watch. It had been about ten minutes, and he counted about 25 people each time. General O was also carefully watching, and he concurred with the numbers Big Jim came up with.

"So when do you want to go in there?" asked Big Jim.

General O replied, "We'll wait until around 3:30 p.m. Things will have gotten a little more routine by then. Will we have to stand in that long line?"

"Nah, I'll get us in when you're ready," Big Jim said. "Do you want Mad Mike and me to accompany you in the building?"

"No," said General O. "After the six of us have entered the building I would like the two of you to go to the exit door and wait there until we come out. When we do, we will be alone. I would like to then quickly walk back to the location where we will be picked up. We can wait there on Fatso and Whalebait.

"Sounds good to me," Big Jim said. "What do you want to do from now until 3:30? And by the way, when do I get my final payment.....the ten thousand?"

General O reached into the breast pocket of his suit and extracted an envelope and handed it to Big Jim. Big Jim looked inside the envelope and started to nod his head and smile.

"We can just sit here and listen to the music from the court house stage. I'm not familiar with that kind of music. What's it called?" asked General O.

"It's called Bluegrass," said Big Jim. "It's very popular around here."

•••

At 3:15 p.m. Big Jim said, "If you want to be in that building by 3:30 we better be headed that way."

All six of the soldiers were patting their feet and tapping their fingers on the table in tune with the music. General O said, "Okay, let us go."

The procession started walking toward the entrance to the Seibert Memorial. A group of 25 had just been admitted. Big Jim's group walked down the waiting line to the 26th person in line, who was a little old lady that stood with a cane. Big Jim said to her, "Good afternoon my dear. I have a group of dignitaries here that would like to view the artifacts. They are on a very limited time schedule, and I wonder if you would be so kind as to allow them to step in front of you in line?" Big Jim held out a fifty dollar bill to her.

The lady quickly grabbed the money and said, "Fine with me. Might not agree with all those behind me."

Big Jim grinned, motioned for the six to step in line in front of the lady, and turned to those behind her and said in a loud voice, "These six people are a very special delegation that have been given permission by Governor Shear to view the artifacts. Please pardon their getting in line ahead of you. It won't slow you down much at all."

Lots of nasty and mad looking faces beamed back at Big Jim, but when the six turned toward them with big smiles and waves the folks just waved back and smiled. Southern hospitality, thought Big Jim, works every time. He and Mad

Mike then headed toward the rear of the building to wait. Big Jim figured the six should be out the back in 15 to 20 minutes.

After seven or eight minutes the line began to move, and 25 people in front of the North Koreans were admitted. The two troopers at the metal detector looked at the next six gentlemen, all wearing brown suits, all Asian, and all with smiles on their faces. The troopers looked at each other with inquisitive looks, and then just shrugged their shoulders. About ten more minutes passed and then the entrance door sprang open and the troopers motioned for those in line to proceed to pass through the metal detector and into the Seibert Memorial. The six were the first to enter, followed by 19 others.

Sheriff Sterling was standing in back of Deputy Kyle Potter keeping an eye on all those entering the exhibit. When the six Asian's came in he was expecting to see Big Jim and Mad Mike following them, but they were not. He immediately became suspicious. The other 19 viewers entered behind the six.

General O was the first of the six in line. As he entered the building he reached into his right pants pocket and felt for the antidote pill called ADX. He felt it. He then reached into his left pants pocket and felt for the vial containing the poison gas called TENX. It was there. Each of his comrades as they entered the building reached into their right pants pocket and retrieved their ADX pill. As soon as all six were in the building they simultaneously placed their ADX pills in their mouths and swallowed. They would then have to wait at least one minute for them to be effective against the TENX.

General O looked at his watch with a sweep second hand as he swallowed his ADX. He then reached into his left pants pocket and retrieved the TENX vial. He had it in his left hand ready to snap the top of the vial and release its deadly fumes. He would do that after all 25 had entered and the entrance door was shut and after at least one minute had passed since taking the ADX.

Bert was watching carefully the Asian visitors. He noticed when they all seemed to put something in their mouths at the same time, but certainly that was not an act to warrant action on his part. He heard the entrance door close.

General O heard the door close and knew that he and the others had taken the antidote. He was just getting ready to break the vial open when he suddenly fell unconscious to the floor......out cold. Each of the other five likewise passed out. The six Asians were all now unconscious on the floor. All 19 of the other viewers started screaming and running to get out of the building. They had no idea what was going on. The state troopers ran to those fallen and tried to revive them, but to no avail. Bert and Kyle both pulled their phones and called for EMTs. Both entrance and exit doors opened.

Big Jim and Mad Mike were startled when the exit door opened prematurely. They were standing about 25 feet from it. When it opened they could see the six on the floor, heard all the screaming, and saw folks running out the door. They quickly left the area headed toward the pick-up point. They knew something bad had gone wrong and that the six would not be going back with them. At least they got their money, Big Jim thought.

•••

Seoyeon Yi did not know how her government planned to use the TENX and ADX, but she knew that very likely many people would be killed. She decided she would have no part of it, and when the government told her to prepare six of the ADX antidote pills she elected to make six that looked exactly like the ADX but were, in fact, 'knock-out' pills. They contained a drug that would within 30 seconds render anyone taking them unconscious for a period of about twelve hours. She reasoned that whoever would have the vial of TENX would also likely be one of those taking the antidote, and since the antidote had to be taken at least one minute before TENX exposure she felt sure that the knock-out pills would prevent the intended poisoning.

Seoyeon knew she was living on borrowed time. Just as soon as the bogus ADX pills were ingested her government would realize that she made the switch. Because Seoyeon was such a fine researcher, she was able to get permission from her government to attend a conference in New York City. She had previously communicated via the internet with colleagues who lived there and would also be attending the conference. She knew this would be her only chance to escape the brutal North Korean government. She made plans for a one-way trip.

•••

Along with the five state troopers, Kyle and Bert rushed to check on the fallen visitors. They had called for EMT's, and they awaited their arrival. Bert went to the first of the six that had entered the Memorial, assuming that he might be their leader. Bert was down on his knees trying to make the person as comfortable as possible when he noticed a small silver vial on the floor beside the visitor's hand. He got the vial and carefully inspected it. It did not seem at all familiar. He made the decision to treat the vial as something that could be very dangerous due to the strange circumstances surrounding the appearance of these six persons. He removed his handkerchief and carefully wrapped the vial in it. He then placed it in his uniform coat pocket.

Sirens were heard outside the Memorial and several EMT's rushed into the building. After carefully inspecting the fallen visitors they pronounced them well enough to be transported to the hospital, and said that their vital signs were very good. Their initial diagnosis was that they had been drugged. All six were then loaded on stretchers and taken to the waiting ambulances for transport to the Harlan Appalachian Regional Hospital. One of the EMTs told Bert that they all seemed to be in a deep sleep and likely would not awaken for several hours. After another half hour the Memorial was again open and the public viewing of the anchor crosses continued.

•••

Big Jim and Mad Mike arrived back at Maggard's Grocery. Fatso parked the minivan around back of the store so it wouldn't be seen. Whalebait took off, since his job was over. Fatso, Big Jim, and Mad Mike entered the store.

Trigger was sitting behind the check-out counter and said, "You got back without the six little men. What happened to them?"

Big Jim said, "We're not real sure. We just know that something happened. The last we saw they were all lying on the floor of that Memorial and it looked like all hell had broken loose. We got out of Dodge ASAP."

Fatso said, "I was listening to the radio, WHLN, and they broke in with an announcement that there had been a disturbance in the Memorial. But about 10 minutes later they announced that everything was back to normal and visitors were pouring through to see the anchor crosses."

"So you just drove their minivan back and parked it around back?" asked Trigger.

"Yeah," said Fatso. "I didn't know what else to do."

Big Jim then said, "Well, our job is done. We did everything we were supposed to do. Mad Mike and I are headed back to Prestonsburg. I'm sure the six little men will eventually show up here to get their minivan. You guys take care." Big Jim and Mad Mike started walking for the door.

Fatso shouted to them, "You know what has four legs and flies?"

They just made it to the door when he shouted again with a chuckle "A picnic table." The door slammed as they went out.

•••

Seoyeon Yi looked at her watch...it was 9 a.m. She then looked out the window of the plane. They were rolling down the runway, gaining speed. The nose of the plane then tipped up, and she heard the landing wheels retract. She leaned back in her seat, closed her eyes, said a little prayer, and then thought 'New York City and freedom, here I come!'

•••

It was about 11:30 a.m. in Pyongyang, and Kim Jong-un sat in his office anxiously awaiting the call from General O at noon. Today would be his big day. Just as soon as he learned that General O and his men had all the anchor crosses and were safely back at the state park he would issue the orders for them to leave early the next morning for Washington, D.C. All this excitement had made Kim hungry. He had ordered three cheeseburgers and two chocolate milk shakes to hold him until after the phone call with General O. If it went well he would then really celebrate with a large meal!

Kim looked at his watch as he took the last bite from his third cheeseburger. It indicated exactly noon. He gulped the last sip from his second chocolate milk shake. This was very unusual. General O had called him every day as scheduled, and always at exactly noon, which was midnight in Kentucky. Could something have gone wrong? Kim waited until 12:30 p.m., and then decided something definitely was not right.

He pushed his intercom and said, "Bring me the morning newspapers....now!"   Thirty seconds later his assistant entered the office with a copy of the morning newspaper. He handed it to Kim.

He found what he was looking for on the third page. The headlines there read: ***Disturbance at the Anchor Cross Festival***. There was a short story, and a photograph that showed six persons lying on the floor of what was said to be the building where the six anchor crosses were displayed in Kentucky. Kim recognized the six. He now knew why he didn't get his phone call. The article said that the six persons mysteriously passed out and were recovering in a local hospital. Kim thought about this for a moment and then again pressed his intercom button and said, "I want Seoyeon Yi brought to my office immediately!" The assistant on the other end of the intercom said, "Yes, Supreme Leader, it shall be done." But it was not. Kim then shot his assistant and threw a fit that would long be remembered by all those in North Korea's government.

Chapter 15

❧ ❧

Harlan County, Kentucky

Bert and Kyle were driving from their office to the Harlan Appalachian Regional Hospital, located only about three miles from Harlan just off highway 421. It was just after 8 a.m. on Sunday. Kyle was driving. Bert said, "Those six little Asians really have me baffled. Their behavior at the festival was very strange, especially being there with Big Jim Owens. He's never been into anything legal in his life. But really all the six did was to pass out in the Memorial, and while strange, that's not illegal. So there are no grounds to arrest them. I just hope they are still at the hospital when we get there. If they've been released we'll likely never see them again, and I do have a few questions I'd like to ask."

Kyle replied, "The docs said that they would likely remain unconscious for several hours. So maybe they got a good

night's rest and will still be there. We'll know soon enough.....
there's the hospital."

Kyle pulled the cruiser into the hospital parking lot. He
and Bert got out and walked toward the hospital entrance.

●●●

The six had been admitted to the hospital and were all
placed in a ward that was unoccupied. They were all by
themselves. They began waking up around 4 a.m. on Sunday
morning. General O, aka James Smith, and Choe Yong-ho,
aka Robert Williams, were the first to awaken. They looked
at one another, and then looked slowly around at their
surroundings. General O said, "Choe, looks like we've landed
in a hospital. I wonder what happened?"

Choe replied, "General, I don't know. The last thing
I remember is taking the pill. Then I woke up here. What
about you?"

"The same," replied General O. "Those pills must have
been switched. I think they were knock-out pills rather than
antidotes."

"So it would seem," replied Choe. "At least it looks like
we're being given good care."

"So far," answered General O. "We'll just have to see what
happens. I know I missed my midnight call to the Supreme
Leader, and I know we failed in our mission. Our futures are
likely not very bright."

The other four then started to awaken, and all six discussed their situation. They agreed that for the moment they would just wait and see what happened. They all agreed not to divulge their true identities. They all lay back in their beds, closed their eyes, and thought about their situation.

At about 7 a.m a nurse came into the ward and caught a couple of the six with their eyes open. She said, "It's good to see you awake. I'll let the administrator know. I think they need to get some information from you. Just enjoy your rest, is there anything I could get for you?"

General O looked at her and said, "Would it be possible to get something to eat and maybe some orange juice and coffee?"

"Coming right up," the nurse replied as she left the ward.

The food and drinks arrived shortly, and all six greatly enjoyed a really good breakfast. Soon after they finished a gentleman wearing a suit entered the ward and said, "Good morning gentlemen. My name is Sandy Mills. I need to get some information from you."

General O said, "Mr. Mills, we are all salesmen from China."

"Do you have hospital insurance and identification I could see?" asked Mr. Mills.

"We have no hospital insurance. We do all have passports. Would you like to see those?" said General O.

"Please," responded Mr. Mills, and he gathered all six passports. "I'll make copies of these and then return them to you." Mr. Mills then left the ward.

•••

Bert and Kyle entered the hospital and went to the information desk to inquire as to where the six men were located. Without names, the person at the information desk said she couldn't help them. Bert then asked to see an administrator. The two were then taken to the office of Sandy Mills.

"Oh yes, I know exactly who you are looking for, sheriff," Mr. Mills said when Bert asked about six men admitted yesterday afternoon. "I just came from their ward. They finally woke up, and we gave them breakfast and then I inquired about their identification and insurance. They said they were salesmen from China. Here are their passports. They said they didn't have insurance."

Bert looked at the passports and said, "Could you please run a copy of these for me."

"Certainly sheriff. Just a minute," replied Mr. Mills as he left his office to make the copies. When he returned Bert took the copies and then he and Kyle left for the ward.

•••

As they entered the ward they noticed that all six of the men seemed to be enjoying themselves. All of them had smiles on their faces, and they were engaged in their own native language conversation. As soon as they saw the two lawmen the smiles faded and they became very quiet. They all looked intently toward Bert and Kyle.

Bert spoke, "Good morning gentlemen. If you will recall, we met yesterday when you were having lunch with Mr. Owens and Mr. Hatfield at the Anchor Cross Festival."

All six nodded their heads in unison.

"And you met my deputy here, Mr. Kyle Potter," Bert said as he pointed to Kyle.

All six nodded their heads in unison.

"The two of us were in the Seibert Anchor Cross Memorial yesterday when the six of you came in. I noticed that each of you seemed to put something in your mouth, and then shortly afterward you all passed out," Bert said.

All six nodded their heads in unison.

"I need to find out what caused you to pass out and what happened to your friends Mr. Owens and Mr. Hatfield," Bert said.

General O spoke, "My name is James Smith. I am a salesman from China. These other gentlemen are also salesmen from China. We were attending a convention in Lexington and ran into Mr. Owens and Mr. Hatfield. They mentioned this wonderful festival that was to be held here in Harlan this weekend and we all modified out schedules to accommodate coming here for it. Mr. Owens and Mr. Hatfield came with us, but have now returned to their homes."

"What was the name of the convention you were attending in Lexington?" asked Bert.

The six just looked at each other.

"I sense something is not right here," Bert replied. "I have copies of your passports and will be checking them out. Are you sure you don't want to tell me the truth about why you are here?"

General O said, "We tell truth. You check us out."

At that time Sandy Mills came into the ward and said, "I'm glad I caught the sheriff and deputy still here. I wanted to ask you six gentlemen how you intend to pay for your hospital visit, since you have no insurance."

"We pay by credit card," General O said. "He reached into his wallet and extracted a Visa credit card from a Chinese bank. He handed it to Mr. Mills and said, "Put the charges for all six of us on that one credit card, please."

Sandy Mills took the credit card and said, "I'll be right back." He turned and left the room with the credit card.

"How did you get to downtown Harlan?" asked Bert.

General O replied, "We followed Mr. Owens and Mr. Hatfield to a store called Maggards, and then got a Mr. Fatso to drive our van into town and drop us off. He was supposed to come back and pick us up at 4 o'clock yesterday."

"I see," said Bert. "And what do you think caused the six of you to pass out?"

"We don't know, Mr. Sheriff," said General O. "It must have been something we ate for lunch from the vendor selling on the street."

Bert said, "Sure strange that it got all six of you at the same time. You sure it wasn't something that you placed in your mouth just after coming into the Memorial?"

"I just put a mint in my mouth. I guess the other five may have done the same. I just don't know, Mr. Sheriff," said General O.

The other five all nodded in agreement at the same time All six had big smiles on their faces.

Mr. Mills walked back into the ward with a frown on his face and said, "Gentlemen, this credit card is no good. Apparently it has been cancelled." He handed the credit card back to General O.

General O said, "I don't understand. It has been used for all our expenses, and it always was good."

"Not any longer," said Sandy Mills. "So how are you now going to pay for your hospital expenses?"

The six looked at each other and shrugged their shoulders.

Bert looked at Sandy Mills and said, "Could you leave us alone to talk for a minute, Mr. Mills?"

"Certainly, Sheriff," replied Mr. Mills as he turned and walked out of the ward.

After Mr. Mills had left Bert pulled up a chair and took a seat in the middle of the ward. Kyle continued to stand beside the door. Bert's chair faced General O. He said, "Gentlemen, I think it's time for a very frank conversation."

General O replied, "Mr. Sheriff, what is a frank conversation?"

Bert said, "One in which we speak the truth. Please allow me to tell you what I believe to be the situation, just based upon my intuition and the limited amount of information I have."

"Yes, please continue with your frank conversation," said General O.

Bert continued, "Okay, to me this is what we have. I do not believe you guys are salesmen from China. You may be from China, but I don't think you are salesmen. My guess is that you represent some organization. And I think that organization wanted to steal the six anchor crosses. For what purpose, I have no idea. I have at least four good reasons to think this. Number one, there are six of you and there are six of the anchor crosses. Number two, when you were admitted to this hospital your clothes and belongings were checked and each of you had a necklace that could have held one of the anchor crosses around your neck. Reason number three is that all six of you entered the Seibert Anchor Cross Memorial Building yesterday at the same time to view the artifacts. All of you then passed out after appearing to put something in your mouths. And number four, you were escorted by Big Jim Owens. I know him to be into all sorts of illegal activity in Prestonsburg. Basically, he's a crook. So all of these things add up and say to me that you were sent here on a mission that was to steal the six anchor crosses. You failed. I feel sure that whomever you work for will not tolerate that failure. My guess is that if you returned to your home you would likely be punished severely or perhaps even put to death. The good news is that you are in the United States. Accordingly, each of you could seek, and I think would be granted, political asylum. You could then seek employment here in this country and begin a new life. But in order to do this you must share with me exactly where you came from and what your mission was. Currently you have broken no laws in our country. I am here to help you. I would ask that you trust me and truthfully share your mission with me."

Kyle then spoke, "Please let me just add that what Sheriff Sterling has just said is absolutely true. I've had the pleasure to know him all my life and to work for him for several years. He is honest to the core. You are very fortunate to have Sheriff Sterling willing to work things out for you. Please trust him."

General O then looked one at a time toward each of his five companions. They each gave a slow nod of their head as he looked at them. General O then slowly nodded his head and said, "You are correct....it is time for us to be truthful. We are not salesmen from China. We are soldiers from North Korea. My real name is General O Kuk-mu. I'll let each of my colleagues introduce themselves."

The other five men each introduced themselves to Bert and Kyle.

General O continued, "Your intuition and observations are correct, Mr. Sheriff. Our Supreme Leader, Kim Jong-un, directed the six of us on a mission to steal the six anchor crosses. We do not know what his intentions were if we were successful. He simply told me he would give me further orders after we had secured the six anchor crosses. Back in my room at the state park in Pineville I have a satellite phone. My orders were to report to the Supreme Leader each day at midnight. I did this until last night. Since he did not get the call, I know he realizes that we failed in our mission. And you are certainly correct; if we returned to North Korea we would likely be tortured and executed. The Supreme Leader does not tolerate failure. We are at your mercy."

All six of the men looked at Bert and Kyle with nods of anticipation.

"Thank you. You have made a very wise decision. I can assure you that you will be well taken care of. Would you now care to tell me exactly what happened yesterday when you came into the Memorial?" asked Bert.

"I will," replied General O. "When we left North Korea we were simply given orders to steal the six anchor crosses. At that time they all were at Dr. Peters' center in Lexington. We tried to steal them from the center, but could not. We were introduced to Mr. Owens, and he said he could bring us to Harlan and to the building where they would all be on exhibit. For an alternate plan to steal them we had been given a vial of extremely poisonous gas and what we thought were six antidote pills. Our plan was to take the antidote pills and then release the gas from the vial. Everyone in the building except us would have been killed. Each one of us would have then grabbed one of the anchor crosses, put it on the necklace we were carrying, and then placed it around our neck. We then planned to leave the building and go back to the state park in Pineville. But after we took the antidote pills we all passed out. Obviously, the pills were not antidotes; they somehow had been switched to some kind of knock-out medicine. That is exactly the true story of what happened."

The color suddenly drained from Bert's face. He realized for the first time since the incident that he had that poison vial wrapped in a handkerchief in his uniform jacket pocket.

He had completely forgotten about it. He reached into the pocket and pulled out the handkerchief. He very carefully then unfolded it until he saw the silver vial. He then said to General O, "Is this the vial?"

The color drained from all six North Korean faces. General O then said, "That is it. Please be very careful. If the gas is released there would be many deaths in this hospital, in addition to our own."

Bert very carefully rewrapped the vial in his handkerchief. He then reached over to one of the beds, pulled off a sheet and wrapped it around the handkerchief, and then got a pillow case and slowly stuffed the wrapped vial into it. He then handed it to Kyle, with a sheepish grin.

"Gee thanks, boss," Kyle said. "What's the plan?"

Bert said, "If you would be so kind, please take it over to the Kentucky State Police. Post 10 is just across the street. Advise them of the extreme hazard it represents and ask them to call in a helicopter to take it to their Laboratory. Their experts will know what to do. I suspect they'll want to somehow analyze and then destroy it."

Kyle started toward the door.

"Don't stumble," Bert said with a chuckle.

"Very funny," replied Kyle as he went out the door.

All six solders looked very relieved.

General O spoke, "What happens now, Mr. Sheriff?"

Bert began, "Technically you are all under arrest. You are each active soldiers from a foreign country here in the United States on a mission to kill many of our citizens in order to steal the six anchor crosses. That's the bad news. The good news is that you have failed in your mission and you have cooperated completely. As I mentioned earlier, I think you should each apply for political asylum. That process could take a while, but I believe it will be granted. Don't worry about your hospital bill, the county will take care of it. But you will have to leave the hospital. I said at the beginning that you are technically under arrest. I can take you to my office and place you in my holding cell. As luck would have it, it has six bunks and no one is currently there. It will just be a place for you to stay temporarily. The cell will not be locked, and you are free to use my private bathroom. It even has a shower, and you are welcome to use it. My guess is that early next week we'll be able to arrange better quarters for you. I will have to confer with Kentucky's Attorney General for advice, but I assure you I'll do everything in my power to assist you in getting political asylum and getting resettled in the United States."

"You are a very kind and considerate man, Mr. Sheriff," said General O. "You know that if our plan had been successful you and all the others in the Memorial building would have been killed. I sincerely apologize, and am so very grateful that it did not happen. We will all try and find some way to repay your kindness and assistance."

All six smiled and nodded their heads in agreement.

"Those are very kind words, General O," Bert said. "But they are not necessary. I'm just trying to do my job and would also like very much to help you guys. You seem to me to be very much worth helping."

"We will do as you say, Mr. Sheriff, and we will try and find a way to repay you some day," answered General O.

Bert then stood and walked around to each of the six and shook their hands. He then said, "Well, if you feel up to it I'll go down and tell Mr. Mills what has transpired. He will then get all your belongings back to you and officially discharge you from the hospital. I'll then borrow a car from the Kentucky State Police and Kyle and I will drive three of you each in the cars to my office. Does that sound okay with you?"

"Yes, yes, Mr. Sheriff. That sounds just perfect. Thank you again," said General O.

Kyle arrived back at the hospital just as Bert had told Sandy Mills what had happened. Bert then asked Kyle to please drive him back to Post 10 to borrow one of their cars. Then they transported the six North Koreans to the sheriff's department. As they walked together into the closed sheriff's department Bert told them about Preacher Puss, and asked them to please respect and watch after the cat. Then, as they entered through the front door they each reached up and gave her a nice pet. Preacher Puss seemed to readily accept the new guests!

After getting all six settled in their new temporary home Bert and Kyle left to go to the morning worship service at New Hope Baptist church. They knew this morning's service would be special.

Chapter 16

Harlan, Kentucky

It was approximately 10:30 a.m. on Sunday. The sanctuary at New Hope Baptist Church had already begun to fill. All the anchor cross owners had been invited by Pastor Bell to attend the morning worship service that started at 11. They had all accepted the invitation. Pastor Bell had reserved the first two rows in the church to accommodate them. In addition, although of a different faith, the Crown Prince from Dubai and his companion, Adnan, had been invited to attend and they too accepted. Their motor home was still parked in the church parking lot, and they had been enjoying all the activities of ACFesII. Raymond asked them to also please sit with the anchor cross owners as guests on the first two rows. All of the guests had arrived early and were seated and enjoying discussing the events of the weekend with each other.

Sheriff Sterling and Deputy Potter arrived and after speaking to, and shaking hands with, all the guests they took seats in the sanctuary. Pastor Bell then walked over to where the two lawmen were seated and sat beside Bert. He asked him how everything was going, and Bert told him what had happened at the hospital this morning and about the temporary six guests in his holding cell. Raymond and Bert continued to talk for another ten minutes. Raymond then excused himself to go greet other parishioners.

Mansour, the Crown Prince of Dubai, turned to look at those seated in the sanctuary. He saw Dr. Randy Peters sitting with Mayor Fred Knapp. Mansour stood and walked back to where the two were seated. He then asked Dr. Peters if he could have a word with him. Randy stood and the two walked over beside a wall in the sanctuary.

Randy Peters said, "Mansour, we are honored that you and Adnan would elect to be with us this morning. I know you are not Christians, but we welcome you as guests with open arms. We are just so pleased you stayed on to attend the festival, and hope everything will continue well with you today and on your return journey home. Is there anything I can do for you?"

The Crown Prince replied, "Thank you Dr. Peters. Adnan and I have really enjoyed the festival and meeting some of the very friendly people here in Harlan. To answer your question regarding if there was anything you could do for me, I would like to tell you that I have decided to do something for you. I do realize the importance of your research on the anchor crosses, and I have decided to make a contribution of ten million dollars to your research program. There are absolutely no 'strings attached', as you westerners like to say. I simply wish to assist you in your efforts. And Adnan and I will plan to stop by for visits with you when we again come to Lexington for the Keeneland horse sales."

"I am overwhelmed," replied Randy. "Words fail me! Ten million dollars will enable us to pursue research avenues that we would otherwise not have been able to explore. On behalf of my university, I thank you from the bottom of my heart. You are so very kind and understanding."

"I think the service is getting ready to start," Mansour said. "Perhaps we had better take our seats. Someone from my office will be in touch with you regarding the logistics of the gift. Thank you again for everything."

The two shook hands, and then embraced. They then took their respective seats.

At exactly 11 o'clock Pastor Raymond Bell stood at the podium. The sanctuary was packed. Several people were standing at the back and along the walls. Raymond said, "Well good morning to everyone. What a wonderful day the Lord has given us. We are blessed beyond measure." All in the audience were nodding, especially Dr. Randy Peters. Several tears flowed down his cheeks. The pastor continued, "This weekend has been one that will long be remembered in the history of Harlan and Harlan County. We have been hosts to thousands of guests here in Harlan, and, through the reports submitted from here by the media, we have been host to the entire world. The magnificent, mysterious, astounding, beautiful, and I could go on with adjectives, golden anchor crosses have generated worldwide interest. I wish I could tell you much more about these artifacts, but the truth is we don't really know very much. Through the efforts of Dr. Randy Peters and his Center for Appalachian Research at the University of Kentucky we have learned a lot about the history of all six anchor crosses. We also know that the gold from which Constantine the Great cast the six artifacts was at one time blessed by our Lord Jesus Christ. Much remains to be discovered about these golden artifacts. And I feel certain that Dr. Peters will discover lots more of their secrets in the future. This morning's worship service is a very special one. We have seated in the front two rows the owners of all six of the anchor crosses. Each of these persons has been introduced to you earlier at the festival, so I won't take the time to repeat that. In addition to the owners, we also have as guests today two very special people. The Crown Prince of Dubai from the United Arab Emirates, Sheikh Mansour bin Ahmed Al Maktoum, and his associate Adnan bin Saeed Al Amin are seated right there. Gentlemen, please wave to the congregation." Mansour and Adnan stood, turned, smiled and waved.

Raymond continued, "It isn't everyday that we have such distinguished guests from the Middle East as our guests here in Harlan." A chuckle passed through the congregation. "We truly thank you for electing to join with us this morning." Pastor Bell then took a seat and the order of worship continued.

The worship service concluded at approximately noon. Afterwards many in the congregation found their way to the front of the sanctuary to shake hands with the various anchor cross owners and with Mansour and Adnan. Mayor Knapp extended an especially vigorous handshake to all the guests and thanked them for their participation at ACFesII.

Sheriff Sterling caught Pastor Bell and said to him, "The more I think about your suggestion the more I like it. I think I'm going to see if I can make it work." Bert was referring to the conversation he had with Raymond just prior to the start of the morning worship service.

Raymond extended his right hand with the thumb pointed up and said, "Go for it!"

Bert grinned and nodded his head affirmatively.

Mayor Knapp then walked up to the sheriff and said, "Bert, everything's going just great now. That was a bit of a scare yesterday when those six people passed out in the Memorial, but we recovered nicely and everything has gone really good. If we can now just get through this afternoon's session and then get those anchor crosses back on the helicopter I'll certainly be relieved."

Bert replied, "Fred, like Raymond said, this weekend will be one that will long be remembered in the history of Harlan. You are to be commended for making it so."

"Thanks Bert, just doing my job," replied the mayor.

"Just as soon as we get this festival behind us I have a lot of information to pass along to you. Hopefully maybe tomorrow morning we can get all caught up."

"We'll do it," Fred replied. "See you at the festival this afternoon."

•••

All of the anchor cross owners as well as the UAE guests left Harlan for Lexington after the morning worship service. All of them had flights out of Lexington Sunday evening. The Sunday afternoon session of ACFesII went exactly as scheduled, and promptly at its conclusion the familiar 'thwap-thwap-thwap-thwap' of the helicopter was heard as it approached the court house helipad. Sheriff Sterling, Deputy Potter, Trooper Ape Cornett, and five other Kentucky State Police officers accompanied the box containing the six anchor crosses to the helipad. Trooper Cornett jumped aboard with the priceless cargo, and the helicopter lifted on its way back to the University of Kentucky.

The Second Annual Anchor Cross Festival was now history.

Chapter 17

⊷

Harlan, Kentucky

After the close of the festival and after safely escorting the anchor crosses to the helipad, Bert had driven to the Kentucky Fried Chicken restaurant located just outside the Harlan city limits on highway 421. He had purchased two of the largest family meal buckets on the menu, and then drove back to his office and presented the food to his six detainees. He kept 2 liter bottles of soft drinks in the office refrigerator, and he gave the six three of these as well. They all stood and bowed and thanked Bert profusely for the food and drink. They then got all settled, distributed the food, and began enjoying it. Bert walked back into his office and sat at his desk.

After thinking for a few minutes and making some notes, he placed a phone call. He talked for about twenty minutes, and then said, "You don't have to make a decision right now.

Feel free to think about it, and give me a call when you've decided." He then hung up the phone after expressing his thanks and saying good-bye.

Then he walked back into the room housing the detention cell and his six 'guests'. Each looked at him with a big grin and nodded approvingly. General O spoke, "That food was super good! We read the writing on the container that said it was 'finger-licking good and made from a secret recipe'. We're not exactly sure what that means, but we approve! Thank you so much Mr. Sheriff!"

"You are most welcome," Bert replied. "That should hold you until tomorrow morning. I'm going to leave the office now. I'll lock the entrance door, and see you in the morning. I hope you all sleep well."

All six stood, bowed, and smiled at the sheriff.

● ● ●

When Bert arrived at his office early the next morning he noticed that Preacher Puss did not greet him as usual. She was not in her bed on the shelf above the entrance door. It was only about 7:30 a.m., and Rosie or Kyle had not yet arrived for work. Bert then noticed that the door going into his office was open, and he guessed that he forgot to shut it when he left last evening. He then walked into his office and then on through the door behind his desk that went to the evidence room on the right and the detention cell room on the left. He turned left in the hallway into the detention cell room. What he saw brought a bright smile to his face. All six of the 'guests' were sound asleep. In the front bunk on the left was General O. He was sleeping on his side with his head on a pillow. His arms were gently curled around a huge mass of gray fur. Preacher Puss, without moving, looked at him with her huge eyes. She started to swish her tail. Bert turned and walked back to his office.

He sat and thought about the days agenda. His phone then rang.

"Sheriff's office, this is Sheriff Sterling speaking." Bert acknowledged the caller and then proceeded to talk for another ten minutes, after which he said, "I cannot begin to tell you how thankful I am for your decision. It is truly an answer to my prayers. I'll start making preparations on this end and look forward to seeing the two of you at 3 this afternoon." He disconnected the phone, sat back in his chair, looked upward and said aloud, "Thank you Lord!"

Just before 8 a.m. Deputies Rosie Cain and Kyle Potter walked into Bert's office. Just as soon as they cleared his door Rosie said, "Where is Preacher Puss?"

Bert replied, "And a good morning to the two of you too. Preacher Puss is safe and sound. Sit down and I'll tell you the story."

Rosie and Kyle both sat down and Bert related what had happened with the six detained 'guests'. Kyle was already knowledgeable.

"So, we have six North Koreans in our holding cell," Rosie said, "but what about Preacher Puss?"

Bert stood and motioned for the two of them to follow

him. He placed his forefinger to his mouth to indicate they should be quiet. The three then walked to the detention cell and Bert pushed the door open so that Rosie and Kyle could see in.

Rosie said, "Now isn't that the sweetest sight you ever saw?"

Preacher Puss remained motionless except for the sweep of her tail, which increased when she saw the three of them looking at her.

Bert gently pulled the detention cell door nearly closed and they all walked back into his office.

"I can't recall seeing a group more contented-looking than those," Kyle said.

Rosie replied, "Yes indeed, and Preacher Puss seemed like just one of the boys!"

"I guess she's adopted them," Bert replied.

"What's going to happen to the six North Koreans?" asked Rosie.

"Don't know yet," the sheriff said, "but I'm working on it."

Kyle and Rosie then turned and walked out of Bert's office back into the entrance room and began their daily routines.

At about 10 a.m. Bert received another phone call. After 15 minutes of talking on the phone he disconnected, stood, and walked into the front office and said to both Kyle and Rosie, "I just got a phone call from the Kentucky State Police laboratory in Frankfort. They told me that initial analysis of the poisonous vial revealed information that would be of great interest to our military. The vial has now been transferred to a U.S. Army laboratory for detailed analysis. They thanked us for getting it to them and said they would keep us updated when they knew more."

"Hopefully some good will come from that," Kyle replied.

"We'll hope," Bert replied. "I could use a little break, and we need to update the Mayor on some things. You up to a visit to Creech Café?"

Kyle grabbed his hat and the sheriff and chief deputy departed.

•••

After briefing Mayor Knapp on all that had happened and then after hearing from the Mayor about how pleased he was with the Second Annual Anchor Cross Festival, Bert and Kyle returned to work.

At 1:30 p.m. Rosie buzzed the sheriff on the intercom and said, "Sheriff, Trigger Green and Fatso Chappel are here to see you."

"Please send them in," Bert replied.

"Good afternoon, Bert," Trigger Green said upon entering the sheriff's office.

"Hey Trigger, Fatso, please pull up a chair," replied the sheriff. "Who's running the store?"

"We got cousin Whalebait to look after things while we came for our visit," replied Fatso.

"What can I do for you?" Bert asked.

Trigger replied, "Well, I'm sure you're aware that Big Jim Owens hired Fatso and Whalebait to taxi them to the festival on Saturday."

"Yep, I did hear that was how Big Jim, Mad Mike, and the six visitors came to Harlan," said Bert.

"Fatso drove the six guys in their minivan. When they didn't show up at the designated time to be picked up Fatso just drove their minivan back to Maggards. We thought they'd show up later to get it, but they didn't. So we drove it over and have it parked in one of your office's parking spaces out back. It's probably a rental, so we thought we'd better get it to you so you could make arrangements with the rental company to pick it up. Here are the keys," said Trigger as he handed the keys to Bert.

"Thanks, Trigger," responded Bert. "I'll certainly take care of it. I don't think you are aware, but we have the six visitors detained here in the back. As it turns out, they are soldiers from North Korea and were here on a mission to steal the anchor crosses. A reporter for the *Enterprise* was in earlier this morning and got the story on them....it'll be in tomorrow's edition. They really seem to be decent people.... just misguided by their government. I'm working now to get political asylum for them."

Fatso's face seemed to light up and he said, "You mean they're all right here now?"

"That's right, Fatso," Bert said, "in my detention cell right through that door."

"Could I see them?" Fatso asked.

"Sure. Come on, we'll walk back there," replied Bert as

he, Trigger, and Fatso walked through the back door in the sheriff's office toward the detention cell.

As soon as General O spotted Fatso he shouted, "Mr. Fatso! So good to see you again. Did you come to tell us another of your stories?" All six immediately stood and bowed to the visitors. Each of the six had big smiles on their faces.

"Well, I'd be happy to do that, but actually I just heard from the sheriff here that you guys were back here and just wanted to say hello," said Fatso.

All six in unison said, "Hello".

Fatso then said, "You know what they call a monkey that sells potato chips?"

Six eager faces looked at Fatso.

"They call him a chipmunk!" said Fatso.

All six roared and doubled over in laughter. Tears poured from their eyes. They clapped their hands. Finally, General O said, "You are the best, Mr. Fatso. Thank you for another excellent story."

Fatso grinned, looked at Bert and Trigger, and said, "You are very welcome. It's really nice to finally find people who appreciate my jokes!"

Bert then said, "Okay Fatso, you're welcome to come back and tell more stories later, but right now I think the three of us have work to do." Bert, Trigger, and Fatso then turned to leave. The six waved to them and all shouted, "Goodbye Mr. Fatso". General O shouted, "Please come back to visit us, Mr. Fatso!"

Fatso turned his head to them and shouted, "Sure will guys, take care."

● ● ●

Bert was sitting at his desk doing paperwork. It was just a few minutes before 3 p.m. when Rosie again buzzed him on the intercom and said, "Your 3 o'clock appointment is here."

"Please send them in," Bert replied as he looked toward the door to his office.

The two Slusher brothers walked into Bert's office.

Gunsmoke and Booger each shook hands with the sheriff and then all three took seats.

"I sincerely appreciate you boys coming over this afternoon. I can't recall when I was happier than when you called me this morning with your decision. Before I forget to tell you, I wanted to make sure you knew that the idea originated from Pastor Raymond Bell. Before church services yesterday morning he and I were discussing the six North Koreans and their situation. He then had the idea that it might be possible for the two of you to take them. After I thought about it, I agreed and gave you the call last night. And then when you called back this morning saying you would do it.... well, it was truly an answered prayer."

Gunsmoke said, "Yeah, Booger and I talked about it last night. We even called ole Gus Richenberger to get his take on it. He seemed to think it would be fine if you wanted it. So we thought about it some more, and then decided to do it. We really don't know what we're getting into, but we do know you are a good man, Bert. We trust you, and if you say it'll work out, then we say let's do it!"

Bert replied, "We are walking a bit on unfamiliar ground here, but I've called several authorities to get their advice, and all thought it would work. Let me just go over one last time what I envision. The six guys will go to your farm to live. You will pay them minimum wage plus provide them room and board. They will work for you, doing everything from working security to doing odd jobs around the farm.... whatever you say. In the meantime, I will proceed with all the paperwork to get them political asylum status. I don't know how long that will take, but when it's finished, and assuming it's granted, they will be free to go their separate ways or to stay with you. That would then be a decision they and you could work out. But until the political asylum comes through they are still officially under arrest. They are just assigned by me to serve their time at your farm. If any of them escaped prior to settlement of the political asylum thing, then that will be my problem, not yours. You have no obligation other than to house them, feed them, and pay them minimum wages for work they do. Is that your understanding?"

Gunsmoke and Booger both nodded affirmatively, and Gunsmoke said, "That pretty much sums it up, sheriff."

Bert stood and walked around to the front of his desk and vigorously shook hands with the two brothers and patted them both on their backs. He then said, "I feel certain this is going to work just great. Let's go now and meet your new hands."

Bert and the two Slusher brothers then walked back to the detention cell. As they approached the door that was ajar they heard cheerful but unfamiliar voices coming from the detention cell. They opened the door and saw a long to be remembered sight. All six of the North Koreans were sitting in a circle on the floor. They had made a small round ball by rolling up a face towel and then putting several rubber bands around it. Preacher Puss was in the center of their circle. One of them would roll the ball across the floor to the other side of the circle and Preacher Puss would chase and grab it in her mouth. The person to whom the ball was rolled toward would then give Preacher Puss a big pet and she would release the ball. He would then take the ball and pass it to another one who would then repeat the process. The six were totally engrossed in this game with Preacher Puss and didn't notice that visitors had entered.

Bert walked over beside the circle of men and said, "Gentlemen, I hate to break up your most enjoyable game, but I have two brothers here that I would like you to meet."

All six then stood. General O had grabbed Preacher Puss and held her gently in his arms as he said, "We play game with Preacher Puss. She enjoy it, and we do too," he said with a big smile. "My name is O Kuk-mu. This is Choe Yong-ho, Bin Yo-han, Ryu Jae-gyu, Seo Chi-won, and Sin Ji-hae," General O said as he pointed to each as he said their name.

Bert grinned and said, "And these are the Slusher brothers, Gunsmoke and Booger."

The six then bowed deeply, smiled, and then formed a line to shake hands with the brothers. General O was the last in line, and when it came his turn to shake hands he shifted Preacher Puss to his left arm and shook hands. The Slusher brothers looked admiringly at Preacher Puss. The cat then did a strange thing. She bolted from the left arm of General O and sprang toward Booger. He grabbed her as she landed against his chest. She looked up with her huge eyes at Booger and started to purr loudly and swish her tail. Booger stroked her gently. Gunsmoke reached over and tickled her neck. The purring got louder. The tail swishing faster.

Gunsmoke said, "I think my brother and I both thought we recognized this cat when we first came in and saw her playing the game with the ball. She's put on a little weight, and looks a bit different, but this cat once lived with us at our farm. Her fur, coloring, and face are unmistakable. And now, as you can see, she remembers us. We called her Smoky, because of the smoke color of her fur. One day she wondered off the farm and we hunted for weeks but could never locate her."

Bert looked astounded, and said, "Well, let me now tell you the rest of the story!" He then went on to tell the Slusher brothers about how the cat was discovered in the burning church and then delivered by the firefighters to his office. He told them how Rosie had adopted the cat, why she had been named Preacher Puss, and how she had adapted to life in the sheriff's office and had even gained quite a reputation for catching crooks. The Slusher brothers were amazed at the story.

After petting the cat for several minutes Booger passed her to Gunsmoke. He continued to pet her, and the cat appeared to appreciate greatly the affection.

Bert then said, "What a coincidence! I can't wait to tell Rosie, and we'll go up to the front office and do just that in a minute, but right now I need to tell the six of you some great news!"

The six looked intently toward Bert.

"These two fine gentlemen, Gunsmoke and Booger Slusher, have agreed to allow you to come to their very nice farm. They will provide you with jobs, will pay you a wage, and provide food and lodging for you. You must remember that you are technically still under arrest until the paperwork goes through for your political asylum. And until that happens, any of you that elected to leave the Slusher's farm without permission would be considered an escaped criminal and when caught would be prosecuted as a felon and would be sent to prison. This would not be pleasant. You would definitely not want this to happen to you. Do you understand?"

General O said, "Yes, we understand. This sounds like a wonderful opportunity for us. We thank you again Mr. Sheriff for your help and understanding. And we certainly thank Mr. Gunsmoke and Mr. Booger for agreeing to do this for us. We will work very hard for them and try and become good citizens of the United States."

Gunsmoke then said, "Thank you. Booger and I think you deserve the opportunity. We look forward to getting to know you and working with you. One other thing I wanted to mention. From what we saw when we came in a moment ago, all of you seem to like cats. Booger and I particularly love animals, and we have quite a collection of them at the farm. We have lots of cats, and you'll all be able to adopt one as your very own if you wish."

All six smiled at Gunsmoke and Booger and then began to clap.

"Not necessary," Gunsmoke said, but the clapping continued.

Bert then said, "Okay, okay. You guys gather your belongings. You're getting ready to head to the Slusher Farm. The brothers and I are going up to the front office to tell Rosie the story about Preacher Puss, aka Smoky. When you have everything and are ready to go just come join us."

The six then started gathering together their meager belongings. Bert and the brothers turned and walked up front. Gunsmoke was now carrying Preacher Puss.

Rosie took one look at the three as they entered the front office and said, "My, my. It looks like Preacher Puss has found yet another buddy."

Bert looked at Gunsmoke and Booger, laughed, and said, "Let me now tell you the whole story! You and Kyle pull up a chair. You both need to hear this." Rosie, Kyle, Bert, Gunsmoke, and Booger all had a seat in a near circle. Gunsmoke continued to stroke a very contented Preacher Puss as Bert told the 'Smoky-to-Preacher Puss' story.

When finished Bert could detect a few tears in Rosie's eyes. Rosie reached over and petted Preacher Puss and said, "Well ole girl, you do have quite a history. It won't be the same around here without you, but I do understand."

The brothers looked at Rosie. Gunsmoke then said, "No, no. You don't understand. We're not taking Preacher Puss. She's established her life here with you and all those in the sheriff's department. We're just very pleased to finally learn what happened to her, and especially pleased that she is so well loved and has such a great home. We will likely stop in every once in a while to visit with her….if that's okay?"

Rosie cheered up immediately. She stood, walked to the brothers and gave each a big hug. Gunsmoke then handed Preacher Puss to her and said, "She's sure one fine cat."

Everyone nodded in agreement. Preacher Puss purred especially loud and swished her tail strongly.

At that moment the North Koreans came bounding into the front office. Each was holding a small bundle that represented his belongings. Bert explained briefly to Kyle and Rosie what was going to happen to them. It then looked like the end of a ball game, where all the players line up to shake hands. The six formed a line and each bowed deeply and shook hands with Rosie, Kyle, and then Bert.

Bert then reached in his pocket and produced the keys to the minivan. He handed these to Booger and said, "You'll find their minivan in one of our parking spaces at the back of the court house. You drive them to your farm. Gunsmoke can drive the car you came in. Kyle and I will come over to visit in a day or so and pick up the minivan. It needs to go back to the rental company."

Bert, Kyle, and Rosie then hugged the brothers as they left the sheriff's department.

Preacher Puss jumped back up to her bed on the shelf above the door. She circled around in her bed a couple of times and then lay down. She slowly closed her eyes while continuing to purr and swish her tail. She was soon asleep.

Chapter 18

Lexington, Kentucky

It was Monday at 6 p.m. Dr. Randy Peters stood in the museum of his Center for Appalachian Research looking at the six magnificent, golden anchor crosses. Each had been placed back in its display case. Randy had spent a good part of yesterday evening at Blue Grass Airport seeing the owners off. He had then come to his office very early this morning to get caught up on all the paperwork that had accumulated while he was in Harlan for ACFesII. Everyone had now gone home for the day, leaving him alone. As he gazed at the beautiful artifacts he thought back to the beginning, to the Seibert anchor cross being found by Kyle Potter. How much had happened since then. Finally, all six of the anchor crosses cast by Constantine the Great in 325 A.D. lay before him. He thought about the fact that the six had been formed from one bar of gold. And that the gold had been blessed, perhaps even touched, by his Lord, Jesus Christ. He thought of all the very mysterious and unexplainable events that were known to have happened to those possessing the anchor crosses. He also considered how the nefarious plans of the evil ones had been foiled. As Randy pondered the power of the Anchor Cross, his attention was drawn to the engraved inscription on each cross. Shining brilliantly in the display lights were the two Latin words he knew so well. Randy was gripped by a realization. It was through Jesus' ancient cross and now these six golden crosses that the ultimate power was unleashed -- the power of peace. Pax Tecum.

Were there additional powers locked in the gold waiting to be discovered? Maybe.

www.ingramcontent.com/pod-product-compliance
Lightning Source LLC
Chambersburg PA
CBHW070016120726
47909CB00003B/952